THE AUTHOR

Jessie Kesson was born Jessie Grant McDonald in Inverness in 1915, and soon moved to Elgin with her beloved mother (she never knew her father). Estranged from many of the family, mother and daughter were forced to live on their own resources, and Jessie's early days were spent dodging the Cruelty Inspector and the rent man, before she was sent to an orphanage in Skene, Aberdeenshire. As a teenager, she entered service, settling in 1934 on a farm with her husband Johnnie, a cottar. Those early years have inspired much of her work: the novels *The White Bird Passes* (1958), *Glitter of Mica* (1963) and *Another Time, Another Place* (1983) – also a prize-winning film, co-scripted by her – as well as short stories such as *Where the Apple Ripens* (1985).

Her writing career was sparked by a chance meeting on a train to Elgin back in the Forties. Some time later – when she received a letter addressed 'Miss (now Mrs) Jessie, on a dairy farm near Old Meldrum', – she learned that her fellow traveller was the distinguished scholar, Nan Shepherd, now writing to encourage her to enter a short-story competition; she won. Dr Shepherd also unexpectedly recommended her to the BBC as an actress – she failed the audition, but went on to script over ninety radio plays for them and to work on 'Woman's Hour'.

Until recently, whether she was writing stories, poems, newspaper features, dramas or novels, Jessie Kesson has always done other jobs. She has been a cinema cleaner, an artists' model and was, for nearly twenty years, a social worker in London and Glasgow. Now a great-grandmother, and the proud owner of a 'scarlet goon' (conferred by Dundee University in 1984), she lives with Johnnie in London, where she is currently writing the story of her remarkable life.

WHERE THE
APPLE RIPENS
& Other Stories

Jessie Kesson

THE HOGARTH PRESS

LONDON

Published in 1986 by
The Hogarth Press
Chatto & Windus Ltd
40 William IV Street, London WC2N 4DF

First published in Great Britain by Chatto & Windus Ltd 1985
Hogarth edition offset from the original British edition
Copyright © Jessie Kesson 1985

British Library Cataloguing in Publication Data

Kesson, Jessie
Where the apple ripens & other stories.
I. Title
823'.914[F]   PR6061.E8/

ISBN 0 7012 0738 8

Printed in Great Britain by
Cox & Wyman Ltd
Reading, Berkshire

For Sharon, Melanie and Joanne
Dear Grandchildren

ACKNOWLEDGEMENTS

'Where the Apple Ripens' was first published in
New Writing and Writers 15, published by John Calder;
'The Gowk' in *Grampian Hairst*, an anthology of Scottish
writing published by the Aberdeen University Press;
and 'Good Friday', 'Until Such Times', 'Life Model'
and 'The Bridge' in *Chapman*. 'Road of No Return' was
originally broadcast by the BBC's 'Morning Story'.
The lines from *The Land* by Vita Sackville-West are
reproduced by kind permission of William Heinemann Ltd,
and Curtis Brown Ltd on behalf of the author's estate.

Contents

Where the Apple Ripens

Never pry
Lest we lose our Eden
Adam – and I –

'On 29 August, 1932. Helen. Aged eighteen years . . .' Her mother's voice drifted to a halt. And Isabel knew it was true. Everything became true when it was read out loud, from the morning paper.

'The funeral's the day, then,' her mother remembered, letting the paper drop from her hands. *That* had been confirmed by the big, black-edged card in the shoemaker's window.

All Friends Respectfully Invited

'I keep forgetting about the funeral,' her mother admitted, gazing out of the window. 'But then, of course, it's been such fine weather. Such fine shimmering days. And I suppose *you've* forgotten all about school!' Her mother whirled round on Isabel, now. 'Your last day at school at that! You can just run up the stairs and look out your father's shirt. His funeral shirt. Bottom drawer down. And bring Davy's Sunday shirt when you're at it. He'll have to go to the funeral. He came up through the school with Helen Mavor.'

Isabel, herself, had shared the same class-room as Helen Mavor. But, being three years younger, and in a junior form, the boundary between them had been unsurpassable. On the rare occasions when it was bridged, the embarrassment of such a unique situation diminished the pleasure of it. She could have died with hot thumping pride when any of the big girls took her hand. Or even said hello! And, if they ever called her by her name, she was so surprised they knew her at all, she couldn't look at them the whole of the day for shyness. Except in peeps. They *know* me, she would think, gripping herself with excitement. I'm *Isabel*! I *am* Isabel. Most of the time she thought everybody else thought she wasn't anybody at all.

Helen Mavor had never spoken to her. Nor she to Helen Mavor. Yet, she remembered her voice. Better than she remembered Else Finlay's voice. And Else, her best friend.

'*Pan loaf*,' everybody said Helen spoke. Because her parents wouldn't allow her to speak Scots. Not even outside school.

'Scots is good enough for everybody else!' they all protested.

'But Helen Mavor is *English*!' Isabel's mother had pointed out. 'At least the mother of her is English!'

That was it, then. Maybe that was why Isabel had always secretly admired Helen Mavor's voice. It spoke the language of the poems she liked to hear. She would write out her transcription as fast as she could, then curl herself round her book, and listen to the top classes saying their poetry.

> Where Alph the sacred river ran
> Through caverns measureless to man
> Down to a sunless sea

But, when Helen Mavor spoke, she would listen harder than ever. Knowing there was a different language, somewhere. And Helen knew it. Another country. And Helen came from it.

> It was an Abyssinian maid
> And on her dulcimar she played
> Singing of Mount Aborrah

'You might bring down that skirt of mine!' Her mother's voice rose from the bottom of the stairs. 'It's on top of your trunk. I'm in the middle of making it down for you.'

That was another thing. Helen Mavor's skirts had always fitted her properly. They were her *own*. Not her mother's made-down.

And Helen wore *shoes* to school. Not just to the kirk, on Sundays. And yet . . . maybe . . . Helen Mavor had never known the challenge of lacing up a pair of boots so tightly, that they looked almost as neat as shoes. She had never known the excitement of announcing with truth . . . 'My boots are needing toecaps again. I'll have to wear my Sunday shoes to school!' And, most of all, had never known the heart-shattering gladness of your mother's small concessions, her brief, unguarded admissions.

'I suppose you can wear your shoes for one day. But I'll never know what you've got against your boots! You've got such trim ankles.'

Had Helen Mavor ever flown down the road, neat and nimble? Knowing from a source that was infallible that she had 'such trim ankles' – worthy of the silver stud sparked splendour with which they were shod.

The colour of her mother's skirt wasn't too bad. But, fingering it, Isabel knew from experience that the 'making down' would be a process that would continue as long as the skirt itself would last. 'A tuck in here. A dart out there!' A conclusion that was a curious mixture of triumph and defeat. 'It's a bit on the wide side for you. But that's a good fault. You're still filling-out.'

Her uniforms lying inside her trunk, ready for the tremendous prospect of 'going out into the world', were a different thing altogether. Unworn by anybody else in all the world. The blue cotton dresses and grey serge aprons 'for the rough work in the mornings'. She buried her nose in the strong, drapery smell that testified to their newness. But best of all, she liked her 'afternoon uniform'. The black dress that wasn't *real* silk. But looked and felt just like it. Her small lace trimmed caps for showing in the visitors.

Good afternoon, Madam. What name shall I announce, please?
Lady –
Lady? *Lady?*

> The Lady of the Lea
> The Lea
> The Lady of the Lea
> The Lea
> Was beautiful exceedingly
> Exceedingly

Strange how small sudden fantasies could take such hold of her. Whirling her round in their own tempo, before releasing her into a kind of emptiness again.

> Exceeding
>   ceeding
>   ly

She didn't mind so much now, about having to go into domestic service. Though it seemed such a short time ago when her future seemed to be simply a matter of chance, like their skipping game.

> Whom shall I marry
> Tell me true
> A handsome young man
> With eyes of blue
> Rich Man!
> Poor Man!
> Beggar Man!
> *Thief*!

Of all the futures Isabel had visualised for herself – and they had been many and various! – domestic service had never come into her reckoning. At least, not until she was old enough to hang around Barclay's Brig, with the girls, home, on 'their day off', from service in the town. They brought traces of its grandeur back with them. In the form of their mistress's cast-off fox furs.

Slung with casual pride across their shoulders. Hand-me-downs that were different, somehow. Signifying a good relationship with their employers. Not one of necessity, like her mother's skirt.

'My *word*!!' her mother had taken to saying lately, 'Jean Craig must be doing *well*! Her mistress is very good to her,' in a tone which implied that she, Isabel, would never do as 'well' as Jean Craig. Not if she lived to be a hundred.

Their world had widened too, for the girls in service in the town. They now knew people Isabel didn't know. The milk boy. The butcher's boy. The grocer's boy. And most fascinating of all, the tram conductors.

. . . They're a right lot, aren't they, Jean? Mind the time my heel got caught in the platform? And yon conductor! The cheek of him! I thought we'd die laughing . . .

Isabel had never set eyes on a tram conductor. But lately, she had an awful longing for a tram conductor to set eyes on her!

Ting-a-ling-a-ling. Laughter you could die of. High-heeled shoes for evermore. Fairy-footed and fox-furred. And glass eyes glistening red across your shoulder.

Their repertoire had expanded too. It was no longer one they shared with her. But something smiling and secret between themselves. Encircling her with rings of sound, but no longer including her.

> Blue heaven
> Just you and I
> When first we kissed
> Neath a moonlit sky

If only they had sung it often enough for her to get the tune, for she could always make up her own words. How she would have blue heavened it, in the school porch on a rainy day, to a captive audience, mystified and admiring.

> Blue heaven
> Just you and me

> Ta rum da dee
> Ta rum da dee

Still. Very soon, now, she would learn all the words, and catch all the tunes. Casting aside the other words, the other melodies, that had notched up the seasons of her childhood to its sum total. Yet, still uncertain. Checking and re-checking. Carrying over old enchantments, not quite erased.

> How sweet the lily grows
> How sweet the breath
> Beneath the hill
> Of Sharon's dewy rose

'Haven't you found your father's shirt, yet?' her mother shouted. 'You're going to be late for school. On your last day, too!'

Although school, itself, had never been very important in her mother's eyes, it was important not to be late for it. Her brother Davy's certificates, nailed up on the walls of his bedroom, testified to years of punctuality and regular attendance. Isabel had never bothered to nail hers up on the wall. Except her *real* certificate for excellence in English. The words were written in gold letters. You could see they were gold, if you looked closely. And, sometimes, depending the way the sun was, you could still see they were written in gold, even from a distance.

> . . . dependent on Thy bounteous breath
> We seek Thy grace alone
> In childhood   manhood   age
>   and death

'You certainly took your time!' Kate Emslie grumbled. 'And that's not your father's funeral shirt! Your mind's always on everything. Except the job in hand! I would have thought there was precious little to sing about on a day like this! There's such a thing as respect!'

'But it's a *hymn*!' Isabel protested. 'That was the hymn we sang for Helen's memorial in the kirk on Sunday.'

That was another thing. They would sing 'By Cool Siloam' for you when you were born. Or if you died young. But just 'The Sands of Time', if you died when you were old. That, itself, might almost be worth dying for, Isabel concluded, having thought it over. All the folk standing up in the kirk, singing just for *you*. And thinking about *you* all the time they were singing. The way you, yourself, had thought about Helen Mavor. Remembering things you hadn't even known were memories. Like the watch Helen had been given on her birthday. The older girls surrounding her admiringly. Yourself, and the other younger ones staring at a respectful distance, in the semi-official capacity allowed on birthdays. It was the first time that anyone had ever worn a watch to school. And, although you hadn't been close enough to set eyes on the watch, you had relayed detailed confirmation of its existence to the other small outsiders.

It's real *gold*! And it's got Roman numbers!

A memory of a memory, maybe. Your mother's watch, locked away in a drawer in the dresser. Signifying the twenty-first year of her life. But isolating it, as if nothing worth confirming had happened to her since. Maybe, maybe the *important* things that happened to folk fell out of time altogether. And flowered into space.

That Sunday in the kirk. They had just finished singing 'Summer Suns Are Glowing'. The day was right for the hymn. And the hymn was right for the day. With the sun streaming in through the stained-glass windows, so that Isabel could have stretched up her arms and pulled down the thick, coloured rays of dust that had gathered above her head. The heat had dragged out the strong sweet smell of the Himalayan cowslips in front of the pulpit,

sending it surging towards her. So near a smell, till she remembered that the cowslips were Himalayan. Far off and foreign. The
thought of that had excited her. Something realised only by
herself. And secret to herself. She had sat down gripping the
secrecy, squeezing it within her. Hard and hot and physical, till it
exploded. Her body had shuddered under its force, before it
trembled down into a release it had never before known.

'I think I have started to have my periods,' she had whispered to
Else Finlay, the moment they got out of the kirk. 'Is there a stain
on my frock?' Else's furtive examination had revealed nothing. So
it was something different after all. A glory. And ordinary people
like Else could find no trace of it.

'You're a woman, now,' her mother had said, without looking
at her. 'You know what *that* means.' It was a statement, not a
question.

'Aye,' Isabel had answered hurriedly, postively. 'Aye. I know.'

Freed from the threat of personal embarrassment, her mother
had relaxed.

'I'll get some material for your towels, next time I'm in the
town. I'll show you how to make them up and sew them. You'll
see to the washing of them yourself. And keep them away in your
chest of drawers. Out of sight of Davy and your father.' For a
second in time, they had become women together. Bound by a
conspiracy of sanitary towels. But Isabel kept the secret of the
Himalayan cowslips to herself.

'Seeing,' Kate Emslie announced, 'as there will not be a hand's
turn done in this house till Isabel clears off to school and you two
clear out for the funeral, Davy might as well saw up a log or two
for the fire.'

'*Me?*' Davy asked, incredulous.

'Aye. You.'

'A *fire*?'

'A fire.'

'*At this time of year?*'

'A fire at this time of year.' Each word Kate Emslie uttered struck at protest, till you thought protest could never recover and rise up again.

'You'd be just as well sawing up a log or two.' Her voice felt its way through the silence. Reaching out for, and trying to touch Davy, again.

'If you ask *me!*' Dod Emslie said, finding his voice again.

'Nobody asked you!' Kate Emslie snapped. 'I was speaking to *Davy!*' she emphasised, believing it herself. For Davy could have disappeared clean off the face of the earth, for all the notice they were taking of him. Yet if Davy ever *did* disappear, Isabel at least, would know where a memorial to him was to be found. Scratched out on the walls of the blacksmith's smiddy.

DAVY LOVES CHRIS B

'*Do* you, Davy?' Isabel had once asked him. 'Do you love Chris B?'

'*Her!*' Davy had scoffed. '*Yon* muckle fat thing?'

'But, DO you, Davy? Not counting she's fat.'

'NO!'

'Not *once* Davy? Not *ever?*'

'Not *once!* Not *ever!*'

Sometimes, sometimes when they got speaking close like that, herself and Davy, Isabel had a right wish to say to him. *Davy.* Davy, if you wasn't my brother, and pretend you hadn't set eyes on me in your life, and you looked up one Sunday in the kirk, and saw *me* sitting there in my Sunday frock. My blue frock with the white collar. Pretend you hadn't seen it before, either! Would *you* have me? For your 'lass', I mean.

But she had never put that question to Davy. He might laugh at her for one thing. Worse still, he might even ask her the same question. And she could never have said Yes. Even if Davy had not been her brother, she could never have felt heart high for him.

She could never have said No, either, though. She knew that well enough. She would just have patted him on the shoulder, and run away. Like she always ran away when she patted him. Pretending it was nothing. Or just something that had happened in the passing.

> Davy E
> Doesn't love Chris B
> Not once
> Nor forever more!

'Keep your eyes on the clock!' her mother warned, 'Instead of wheebering away to yourself there! You're going to be late for school. And this is your last day!'

'You promised you wouldn't wear your coat, today. If it was fine!' Else Finlay accused, when Isabel caught up with her at the crossroads.

'You promised! And it's going to be a scorcher!'

'I know,' Isabel submitted humbly. 'But I forgot. I just clean forgot.' She emphasised the lie. It wasn't that she had forgotten, it was just that her mother had remembered.

'Here's your coat!' her mother had shouted, a minute before Isabel had got out of sight of the house. 'Fine day or no fine day,' she had insisted, stifling Isabel's rising protests. '*You* are wearing your coat! Else Finlay can run around the countryside exposing herself if she likes! But *you* are going to wear your coat!'

Not once. Not ever. Had Isabel been allowed to walk the world the way she wanted to walk it . . . Wear your cardigan! It's no day for thin shoes! Get your hair back into its plaits again! Flying all round your face like that! Gathering up the dirt . . .

Nobody in all the world knew the *real* Isabel. The Isabel that lurked somewhere within the long coat, tacketty boots and tight plaits. The only thing that made the world's ignorance tolerable was the secret surprise Isabel had in store for it!

'You're laughing at something!' Else accused her. 'Anyhow!' she boasted, as if she were a different species altogether, 'I'd just *melt* if I'd to wear a coat on a day like this. It's going to be a sizzler!'

It would and all. For Ben Achie lay light and near in the sun. Full of fields that danced and ran as fast as herself and Else, with the sun dancing along them. But you could lose your way to Ben Achie, Isabel remembered, when the sun was off. And twenty miles wouldn't bring you up to it.

The women waiting for the bus at the crossroads were full of the funeral. And of the pity of it. Helen Mavor had been young, they said. And strong. She had survived the birth. But would neither eat. Nor try to eat. You could die of course, of a broken heart. Or of shame, itself, just.

'And it could just as easily have happened to *you*!' The joiner's wife predicted, suddenly aware of Isabel. 'So you can wipe that grin off your face. And just you mind on that, my lady!'

O, for the bravery that Isabel regretted she was too young to possess. Except, of course, the kind of bravery that spurred her imagination, at the oddest times, and in the strangest places. Taking the illicit short cut through the barley field, with the wind in her face, fighting against her, and the bearded barley conspiring against her, and closing in on her, stinging her cheeks, and her mind, into some recollected spirit of defiance.

> I wad hae made a wudden horse
> Oot o ilk aiken tree
> And slashed the rowans intae spears
> For sake o chivalrie

You are, her mind attacked the joiner's wife, just a nasty old bitch! You'd like fine for such a bad thing to happen to me, because you don't like us. Not since my mother had bravery, and told you what to do with your planks that got all warped and ruined our hen-house. You was just too greedy to wait till the wood got ripe and could shrink no more. And!!!

I *will* have *The Garden of Allah*! Her mind flew forward to some possible future attack on Miss Merit, the mobile library lady. I'm *not* too young. I know what I want to read. I have read *Masterman Ready*. Ages ago. And I just hated it! So thank you, Miss Merit. But I'll just hold on to *The Garden of Allah*, if you don't mind!

'So you're going away to service in the town, Isabel!' Kate Riddrie said. Launching the others into a concentrated attack.

She'd have to *work*, they said. By God, she would! No more time to sit and scratch herself. For they knew what was what! Once the young ones got to the town, they went all to hell, just! And, if they didn't do *that*, they got too big for their boots altogether!

Take Jean Selby. Her that got married on to a bricklayer, last month. The bragging and boasting that was on *her* had to be heard to be believed! No more paraffin lamps for yon one. GAS! If you please. No more running outside to the water closet. Emptying pails, and all that soss! She'd just to pull a chain, now! To hear *her* speak, you would have thought she'd got married to Sir Robert MacAlpine himself! Not just one of his bricklayers.

You couldn't blame them altogether, Nell Phillips ventured. Not for wanting things a bit easier, like. Although, it was a queer thing, in spite of the gas, and the inside lavatory, the town way of life could never have been the way for Nell Phillips, herself. Wasn't that the queer thing?

It could never have been the way for her mother, either, Isabel knew, as the small images of her mother's life fluttered to the surface of her mind.

The surprised triumph in her voice on churning days when she'd call out, 'The butter's come! It's come at last.' As if, after all the years, she hadn't expected it to 'come' at all. The absorbed precision with which she patterned the butter into small intricate whirls and twirls, that none but her family would ever admire.

The careful concentration with which she'd bend over the lamp. Trimming it down to a minute perfection, as if aware that the giving of light lay within her hands.

They had it too easy altogether, Lil Eadie concluded. Those that went to the town. Take Helen Mavor, now. Though one should not speak ill of the dead. And her not buried yet. *She* had paid in full for what she'd done. Poor thing! She'd always had everything that money could buy. No wonder she got into trouble. If it had been some poor farm-kitchen girl, you could have understood it, poor bitches! A bit of toss and tumble was all *they* had to look forward to! And, even then, the way they carried on up in the farms was a perfect disgrace, just!

'Lil Eadie was quite right!' Else panted, as they ran towards the school. 'Our servant's just like that. Always skirling with the horsemen up in the dark in the loft. And you know fine what they're up to!'

Isabel *did* 'know fine'. But, another knowing, and one outwith her experience, seized sudden hold, carrying her body up into some dark hay-loft, and placing it under, not one horseman, but all the horsemen that ever was. She could have deserted Else there and then, and gone flying up to Corbie's Wood, to ease the agony that her mind's unexpected vision had thrust upon her unsuspecting body.

'They must be a *terrible* lot, then,' she agreed with Else. Glad that the trembling hadn't reached her voice. 'They must all be disgusting, just!'

'But the Egyptians overtook them encamping by the sea beside Pi-hahiroth before Baal-zephon. And the pillar of cloud went from before their face and stood behind them.'

The dominie slammed the bible shut, and leaning on his elbows on the high lectern, cupped his face in his hands, and surveyed the class in silence.

'Watch *out*!' Isabel whispered in warning to Else. 'He's got on his black suit!'

'Not the mark of Cain!' The dominie's voice cracked through the silence. 'Though there is no doubt in my mind, that a few of you will end on the gallows! But the stoop of the farm labourer is early upon you. Square up your shoulders, men!'

'I *told* you,' Isabel confirmed, bolting upright in her form. 'He's always in a bad mood when he's in his black suit.'

'The inspector must be coming the day,' Else whispered.

'When I—sa—bella Emslie condescends,' the dominie broke into Else's speculation, 'to give us her *undivided* attention . . .'

A bad start to her last day at school. A day on which some quarter was usually allowed. A day when small, personal compulsions had to be acted out and inanimate things took their ultimate revenge. Desks, walls, and stones touched in wordless gestures of farewell.

'You will have an extra hour at dinnertime,' the dominie said. 'Do any of you possess a time-piece?'

'It's not the *inspector*, Else!' Isabel remembered. 'It's the funeral. He'll be going to Helen Mavor's funeral. I forgot all about that.'

'Do *you* possess a time-piece, I—sa—bella? I thought not,' the dominie said, answering his own question. 'The acres at Slack-o-Linn, all eighty of them, would not rise to a time-piece.'

Cowards! All of them! Giggling audibly under the dominie's protection. The way Isabel, herself, became a coward, when the dominie made a joke about somebody else. The force of her rising anger confirmed her faith in her own strength to fell them *all*, the moment they got outside. One by one. Or altogether if need be!

'Silver or gold have I none,' the dominie said, his watch glinting and jangling in front of her eyes. 'But this time-piece is above price. I leave it in *your* custody, I—sa—bella . . . *I—sa—bella*!'

'Isabel's got the dominie's watch!' the cry rose in the playground.

> 'The dominie's watch!
> The dominie's watch!
> Isabel's got the dominie's watch
> On a cold and frosty morning.'

The Loch Wood had always been the older girls' favourite hiding place. The privacy they scrambled towards, now enclosed them. Here, they could see yet not be seen. Utter, yet not be condemned out of their own mouths. The 'extra hour' began to draw them into its passing minutes, the way the funeral was beginning to draw the mourners far down the Loch Road.

'Helen Mavor's baby is going to be baptised at the funeral service,' Liz Aiken said. 'At the head of Helen's coffin.'

'It's a lie!' Isabel protested, bursting out from the bewildered silence. Birth and death were such opposite things. You couldn't fuse them together and make them into one! 'By Cool Siloam' was for *birth*. 'The Sands of Time' was for *death*. You couldn't harmonise such divided melodies. 'We sang "By Cool Siloam" for Helen's *death*,' she reminded them, trying to formulate it. 'They can't sing it for the baby's *birth*,' she added, as if the baby had missed out on something.

Never had Isabel ran so fast up through the Loch Wood, nor stumbled so often in the bracken, nor picked herself up so soon. Never had she climbed the tree so high, nor swung so sure and careless along its branches. 'By Cool Siloam' singing inside her head, and she couldn't get it out of her head, nor could she slow her body's movements down into its rhythm, but speeded up the lament it was, till it became a paeon of praise for being alive itself.

'Jump! Isabel!' The girls' voices rose up to her in warning. 'It's the dominie! He'll see you swinging up there. He's on his road to the funeral.'

She could see the dominie now. Striding far down the Loch

Road, in his long, black elder's hat and long-tailed coat. A sight familiar enough in the kirk on Sunday, but alien and out of context on a bright week-day of harvest-time. A *special* occasion this, though. And, maybe, she thought, one worth dying for too. The dominie walking the long road to her funeral. Announcing from his high lectern: Owing to the sudden and tragic death of *I—sa—bella Emslie*. At an age when she was about to cross the threshold of womanhood. It was not to be. *Thy* will, not *ours*, be done. The school will be closed. Let us pray.

I spy! The impulse to shout, and startle the dominie below, almost overcame Isabel. 'I spy,' she said, but in a whisper that couldn't stir the wood into some ghostly echo.

'It was some man in the town, that got Helen Mavor into trouble!' Jean Begg was saying, when Isabel got down to the others again. 'A *married* man at that, my mother said,' she emphasised. Her voice containing all her mother's condemnation.

'My mother *saw* him, once,' Meg Allan remembered. 'At the bus stop at Mealmarket Street,' she added, placing the villain of the piece in a landmark that was familiar to them all, and giving him immediate, horrific reality. 'He'd got a black moustache, and a pair of yon brown suede shoes.'

'Our Davy had a pair of them, once,' Isabel volunteered. Knowing nothing about the man, but something about suede shoes. '"Never again" my mother told Davy. The toes got all shiny and scuffed.'

Aware that her contribution, wordlessly received, had added nothing to the intriguing topic, she began to expound with a vehemence that she knew would 'get' them!

'And anyhow! I'd never have a man with a black moustache. Nor brown suede shoes either! Never!'

'What kind of man would *you* have, Isabel?' They asked, beginning to crowd round her. 'Tell us, Isabel,' they pleaded. 'Go on! Do tell!'

'Tall. Dark. And handsome!' Meg Allan prompted.

Too vague a description altogether. And one that never came to life in Isabel's mind. Not the way a boy might smile. Sharp and sudden in the passing. Or his hair quiff up. Leaving her mind and body quivering with the small surprise of it. Or like times when the tenor, standing opposite her in the kirk choir, sang

That to perfection's sacred height
We nearer still may rise

She could have transported him clean away, to some dark, warm isolation. Certain of finding with him, the perfection his voice had promised.

'It's Alan Soutar!' Else prompted. 'Isn't it, Isabel? You love Alan Soutar!'

Not now. Not any more. Though time was when the briefest physical contact with Alan Soutar, like handing him a book, or skirting against him in the passing could induce a fork flashed flame of mind and body, in confirmation of which, was there for all the world to see, scrawled across the lavatory wall:

IE   LOVES   AS

It was on that day when a note from him, passed from desk to desk, unread by the couriers, with that integrity which governed such rituals, exhorted her to 'Give me a ride in Corbie's Wood', that revulsion had overcome her. Inexplicable revulsion. She, who would willingly have lain down in the dark, with a thousand horsemen! Maybe. Maybe it was just the wording of the request that had repelled her, and sent her flying to the girls' lavatory, to erase all trace of the fact that IE had once loved AS.

'She doesn't *know*!' Meg Allan said. 'She doesn't know the kind of man she would have!' But, she was beginning to grope for his identity in her mind. And the quest for him had already begun; a silent sharp scrutiny of the few boys and men, within her limited knowing.

Oh I'd know my love
By his way of walking

'She doesn't *know*!' Meg Allan insisted, as they began to scramble down the slopes of the Loch Wood. 'She doesn't even know, *herself*!'

And I'd know my love
By his way of talking

The heat had gone out of the day. The sun was going down slowly, and only slowly was the day going down after it. Ben Achie that had looked so near, and within hand's touch, in the morning, was blue now, and far. And twenty miles wouldn't bring you up to it. Yet, Isabel remembered, her mother had said when *she* was young, and went to be a servant in the south, Ben Achie had walked with her, all the way to the Pentland Hills.

'See you on Monday morning!' Else said, when they reached the crossroads. 'If it's hot like today,' she reminded Isabel. 'Don't wear your coat. And I won't wear mine.' Her instructions carried themselves across the barley field. For they had always kept up a running conversation, till they lost sight of each other.

'*Promise*!' Else's voice echoed on the air.

'Promise!' Isabel echoed in reply.

It was only when she turned up her own road that Isabel remembered she wouldn't see Else on Monday. Or on any other morning. The ritual of last day at school, which gave it implicit finality, had been submerged. Cancelled out by Helen Mavor's funeral.

On Monday morning, the dominie would stand behind his lectern, telling how the Israelites had managed to cross the Red Sea. They would cross it all right, Isabel knew. God and the dominie would see to that! They had always been on the Israelites' side. But Isabel would not be there to witness and confirm the achievement, and so the Israelites would be doomed to wander forever through her mind, in a pillar of cloud. Somewhere between Pi-hahroth and Baal-zephon.

The feeling of anti-climax that had overtaken Isabel increased when she reached the house, to find Davy, still in his funeral suit, pumping up his bike.

'You're *going* some place, tonight, Davy,' she accused. 'Some place special. You've still got on your best suit!'

'I *could* be,' Davy admitted, grinning. 'I could be that!'

'*Where*, Davy?' She pleaded. '*Do* tell!'

'If I told *you*.' The grin spread itself across Davy's face, convincing her it was some place *good*. 'If I told you, you would be as wise as *me*, then. Wouldn't you, now?'

'*Where*, then, Davy?' she insisted. Hating the urgency of having to know, and the envy she heard in her own voice. For Davy was allowed to walk a wider world than herself. Down to the blacksmith's forge on a Saturday night. Off to the town with their father, now and again, to sell a bull calf, or buy a heifer calf. Away some nights free-wheeling down the brae on his bike. 'After some lass or other' as their father put it. Davy had never to create another world for himself. Had never lain beneath the blankets, awestruck in Xanadu. Or trembled in the ice-cold immensity of a cavern 'measureless to man'.

'I don't care anyhow!' Isabel assured him, shrugging, and beginning to pass on. 'I don't care *where* you're going tonight. Because I'm going away *myself* soon. Not just for an hour or two. Or half a day! But for a long time. And further than *you've* ever been!'

> Lord I'm one
> Lord I'm two
> Lord I'm three
> Lord I'm four

> Lord I'm *five hundred* miles
> From
>   my
>   home

'Beldie!'

'What is it, now?' Isabel turned, stiffening with suspicion. For Davy only called her by her family 'pet name' when he wanted something. 'What do you want *this* time!'

'Beldie. Will you deliver the blacksmith's milk, for me the night? You're always shouting to go other nights,' he reminded her.

True enough. Isabel had always loved an 'official' visit to the blacksmith's smiddy. To discover who now LOVED whom, from the names that flickered across its firelit walls.

'But you never let me go *other* nights!' she remembered. Past injustices rankling within her.

'Because you're too *young* other nights!' Davy pointed out. Logic and patience beginning to desert him. 'You know fine what I mean, Beldie!' he said, when the laughter had left her.

'On one condition, then!' she stipulated, restored to good humour again. 'If you tell me where you're going tonight.'

'To a ball,' Davy admitted. 'To the harvest home ball.'

'Did Mother say you could?' Isabel asked. Hoping somewhere, that Mother had said *no*!

'Not yet,' Davy confessed. 'I'm waiting for the right time to ask her.'

'I'd dive *right in*, Davy!' Isabel advised. 'I'd dive right in and ask, if I was you!'

'I might. In a wee while,' Davy agreed.

'I wouldn't even wait a wee while!' Isabel urged out of past experience. She, herself had stood so often within that precarious moment of time. Before *no* was irrevocably uttered. And *yes* was still an entrancing possibility. '*I* could ask for you,' she suggested, willingly enough. It had always been easier to ask favours for other folk. Besides, it always put them in your debt.

'Some hope,' Davy said. His voice holding none. 'You know *fine* what she'll say to that!'

'Has Davy not got a tongue in his own head?' Isabel remembered, putting on her mother's voice.

'Do you know something?' Davy asked, staring at her, as if he had just discovered something himself. 'You looked just like Mother for a minute, there!'

'I'm like Father!' Isabel protested. 'Everybody says! Has he got back from the funeral, yet?' she asked, remembering.

'Not yet,' Davy said. 'He went back to the vet's house for a funeral drink.'

'That's your chance, then, Davy!' Isabel urged. 'You should ask Mother about the ball, now! When she's on her own. Before Father gets in to side-up with her!'

'I can't,' Davy said. 'Mother isn't in, either!'

'The Rhode Islands are laying away from home,' the note under the milk jug told Isabel. 'Have gone up to Crombie's Wood to look-see. If your father gets home before me start getting the supper have finished your skirt try it on with the house all to yourself.'

Isabel's skirt lay on the floor, as if her mother had flung it from her, in her haste to be gone. Her unwashed cup and saucer were still on the table, and the teapot still felt warm. Although it was empty, the kitchen had a spell of livingness over it. The way the three bears' cottage might have seemed to Goldilocks, when she stood on its threshold, aware of her own intrusion.

'Where on *earth* has your mother got to, then?' Her father's voice behind her, echoed Isabel's own resentment, his gaze searching the kitchen, as if his wife might be hiding somewhere within it.

'To Corbie's Wood,' Isabel told him.

'To Corbie's Wood? At this time of day? Away up to Corbie's Wood!'

Her father's bewilderment lent distance to the journey. And cast remoteness over the traveller

> . . . faithless is she
> She left lonely forever
> The kings of the sea

'Has *Davy* gotten back yet, then?' her father asked, as if Davy, too, might have disappeared.

'He's round at the back,' she told him, 'pumping up his bike.'

'Still kirning away with that bike of his, then?' her father grumbled. 'I would have thought he might have made a start to scything the inroads. Seeing the weather's holding up like this!'

Davy would never get to the Harvest Home Ball, now. Isabel knew. Her father would never let such fine harvest weather, go wasted by.

'Aye. But the weather's holding up just grand!' her father confirmed. 'Look-see, Beldie!' he urged. 'Just you take a look over at Ben Achie, there! Not a speck of mist on it. I've never seen the Mother Top so clear as 'tis the night!'

> Ye mountains of Gilboah

Always Isabel had loved the proud, implacable sound of those words that evoked a vision of some bearded patriarch, bowing to the mountain. Honouring it. But yet commanding it

> Let there be no rain
> Neither let there be dew

'Well then! Beldie lass!' Sudden and jovial, her father whirled round on her, rubbing his hands in anticipation. 'What's about some supper, then? You'd better be getting your hand in, eh? Going away to the town, to service, and all! Next week, is't? Next week, sometime?'

'On Monday!' Isabel reminded him. Resentful that he had forgotten. 'This first Monday.'

'You'd better give Davy a cry,' he said, turning to look out of the window again. 'We'll need to make a sharp start, if we want to get through with the cutting of that corn. Aye, will we. Me and Davy.'

'You've got to get ready for your supper!' She shouted to Davy, waiting till he reached the door; to hiss with a vindictiveness that took herself by surprise. 'And you'll never get to the Harvest Home ball, tonight! I know that much!'

'Have you not got a start to your suppers, then?' The attack in Kate Emslie's voice, took them by surprise, and disarmed them.

'Where did you get to, then?' Dod Emslie asked. But he had already lost the first round.

'You know fine where I was!' Kate Emslie snapped, clamping the basket of eggs down on the table. 'I left a note. I was away to Corbie's Wood.'

To Faery Lands Forlorn, Isabel knew, struck by the bright expectancy of her mother's look, searching the kitchen, as if she hoped for some transformation. Her hair, in some wild escape from the bun that usually held it tight with such severity, ruffled in curls round her forehead. She must have been pretty once! Isabel realised with small, pleased surprise. Maybe Davy was right, after all! Maybe she *did* look a bit like mother.

'Was it worth it, then?' Father asked. 'This trek away up to Corbie's Wood?'

'Well worth it!' Kate Emslie confirmed. 'I *knew* the hens were laying away. I found nine eggs up there. And all sound. At least sound enough for baking with,' she qualified. 'I see you haven't changed out of your best suit, Davy!' Her vision had dimmed down to the level of the kitchen again, and she was noticing at last.

'The sooner he does *that*, the better!' Dod Emslie agreed with her. 'We'd maybe get a start to some work, then!'

Speak, Davy. Speak now. Isabel exhorted him silently. Or *forever* hold your peace.

'I was going out, the night,' Davy said, as if in answer to her wordless plea.

'Out?' Dod Emslie spoke as if Out was a place beyond their ken. And Kate Emslie's voice an echo from its farness. '*Out?*'

'To the Harvest Home Ball,' Isabel blurted. Lest Davy would never find the words for himself.

The reaction began to whirl round the kitchen in dark circles of sound. A Harvest Home Ball on a night like this! And a funeral day at that! For, who on *earth* had disrespect enough to hold a ball at such a time? It showed you just what folk were coming to. Though they themselves, had not yet come to that. Nor would they ever countenance the like! If Davy thought, that for a single minute, they would allow ... 'then Davy better have *another* think!' Kate Emslie warned, halting the tempo.

'I didn't mean to tell, Davy.' Isabel's voice broke through an appalled and quivering silence.

'You blabbering bitch!' Davy said, without looking at her. 'You big mouthed mare!'

'Language!!' their father warned him. 'Just you guard your tongue, my Mannie!'

'I didn't mean to, Davy,' Isabel pleaded. 'It just came out!'

'You never *mean* to do anything!' Davy said, grabbing the saw from the porch shelf, and turning to look on her before he slammed the door behind him. 'But you go and do *everything* just the same!'

'Everything,' her mother added. 'Except make a start to getting the supper!'

'Aye,' her father sided with her mother, 'Beldie's whiles some quick with that tongue of hers.'

The treacherous, wayward tide of family opinion had begun to turn against her.

'I didn't *mean* to, Davy!' she shouted against the high scream of the saw. 'Davy!' she urged. 'Do you *know* something. Davy? I got the dominie's watch the day! It was *gold*, Davy. Real gold.'

'That's nothing!' Davy said, moved into speech at last. 'That's nothing, just. The dominie was always giving his watch to some lass or other.

'*I* never saw him do it before!' Isabel protested.

'You wouldn't see everything!' Davy assured her, calmly, bending to pick up the sharpening stone.

'I would have seen that!' Isabel insisted, in a desperate awareness, that some important part was falling out of her day. 'I *would* have seen that. And remembered.'

Maybe, maybe she didn't see everything! Come to think of it, she had never really known Davy 'young'. Strange to think that Davy's boyhood was held within the dominie's memory.

'Your brother!' he had once chided her. 'Your brother could have given me that square root, in the time that you are fickering about there, sharpening that pencil! I doubt, though,' he had qaulified, 'if David ever truly comprehended that splendour

> that falls
> On castle walls
> And snowy Summits.

But the thing she had just seen, too elusive for words, clamped her mind down in a small tight vice of pain. The way Davy had gripped the back of the chair, till his knuckle bones showed white. His wrists were awful thin, she had realised. Davy's wrists are awful thin, she had thought, staring.

'I just *hate* the sound that sharpening stone makes!' Isabel burst out, at last. 'It cuts me all up into little bits!'

'A pity, that!' Davy said, the grin beginning to spread across his face. 'A pity it didn't cut your tongue into little bits as well!'

You're *right*, my boy!
Hold up your head.
And look like a gentle man, Sir!
Now tell me who King Davy was
Now tell me if you *can*, Sir!

'You'll get your legs cut off and all!' Davy warned her, 'if you keep dancing round the saw, like some daft thing!'

King Davy was a mighty man!
The King of the Cannibal Islands
He ate his only daughter Jean
And was banished to the Highlands!

Now that her father and Davy had left for the fields, Isabel had a large, but illusory sense of freedom.

'You can get on with the pressing of your skirt, now,' her mother suggested, 'seeing as we've got the house to ourselves for a while.'

But I would rather wear a skirt of flannel. Red and wide. And a petticoat, white and frilled, flouncing beneath it. And I would run barefoot from Slack-o-Linn to Corbie's Wood. Past the smiddy. And past the kirk. Casting my eyes on none! But, knowing all had cast their eyes on *me*. And *blinded* for it! Until Cophetua broke the spell. And rang the silence with a remembered vow

This *Beggar Maid*
Shall be my QUEEN!

'You'd make a far better job of that skirt,' her mother advised, 'if you'd press it on the wrong side. The seams won't show up, that way,' she added, shattering the crystal ball, with an instinct that was almost unerring. 'It doesn't look too bad, now that you've pressed it,' she conceded, allowing neither time nor desire to gather the shattered fragments together again. 'I think I've got a blouse upstairs somewhere, that might go well with it. Pick up the blue check in it, like. The thing is . . .' Her mother paused and surveyed Isabel with a curiosity that began to embarrass them both. 'The thing is,' she repeated, turning away to take the kettle off the hob. 'You're a lot fuller in the bosom than I am. Or ever I was.'

Isabel had never dreamt of 'undressing' her mother, before. Being fine pleased to think that there was nothing at all under her mother's tweed skirt and cotton overall – *other* people's mothers were different, of course, as she had discovered from Else, on one unforgotten day.

'I know fine when they're doing it in bed at night,' Else had confided. 'I can hear them starting to grunt.'

'Mine don't!' Isabel had protested. Shocked beyond all reasonableness. That her parents 'did it' at all, was something that had to be accepted. But never quite condoned. 'They don't grunt though!' she had insisted. 'They just don't *ever* grunt!'

'Keep your hair on!' Else had advised. 'I never said they did. But *everybody* does something. Our servant told me she keeps her eyes shut. Because she doesn't like to look!'

'Dear God,' Isabel had prayed. 'Please help me when the time comes. Because I won't know whether to keep my eyes open or shut.'

'Anybody home?' Lil Eady shouted, pressing her face against the kitchen window.

'For God's sake, Beldie!' her mother urged, 'get that ironing board out of sight. We don't want *that one* carrying our business all round the countryside.'

'That's surely the skirt of your best costume!' Lil Eady accused, pouncing on the skirt. 'Lord, Kate, you're not going to start showing your knees!'

'I'm making it down for Beldie –' Kate Emslie snapped, retrieving the skirt. 'It's on the tight side for me now. And Beldie's filling out.'

'It's to be hoped that she's not filling out like some I could mention in this parish.'

'It's to be hoped not, Lil,' Kate Emslie said.

'Unless, of course,' Lil repeated, settling herself back, and spreading herself out into an ease that betokened a lengthy stay, 'unless, of course, *she* is beginning to fill out, like *some* I could name, in the Parish.'

'It is to be hoped not, Lil.' The chill in her mother's voice would have frozen anybody else into silence, Isabel knew. Except Lil.

'Others have hoped that!' Lil pointed out, warming to her subject. 'I bet you the vet's wife hoped the self same thing! And look you what happened to her Helen! Not, mind you,' she emphasised, 'but what yon lass of hers just *asked* for trouble. With yon high heeled shoes she always wore. The wonder to me was she never broke her neck in yon things. And stockings so thin, you could almost see the hairs on her legs through them!'

'Helen Mavor is dead!' Kate Emslie said. 'And buried now,' she added, reminding herself of something she should not have forgotten.

It was just that. Just being buried, that made death so ominous to Isabel. If one could lie, like Sleeping Beauty, encased in glass, and visible, for a hundred years, death might just about be acceptable. For one could look upon you then. And speak to you. And keep you in mind. Could even resurrect you. It was the end of *being* that was outwith her comprehension – if death *was* universal, that was! – Isabel had a feeling it might not be! Death couldn't remember everybody in the world. Surely one or two *might* escape, forgotten, from its clutches. O King Live Forever. She had a feeling, that *she* might just be lucky enough to be one of those whom death forgot.

'The mother of her was in a terrible state,' Lil Eadie was saying. 'Terrible, just. I heard tell of it from big Bill Mackie. You mind on him, Kate? He retired from the police. O, a good five years ago it would be, now. And he's never missed a funeral since! They say he dives for the local paper first thing every morning, to see if he can find some funeral or other to go to.'

'Seeing us all under, like?' Kate Emslie commented.

He had nothing better to do! Lil supposed. All irony lost on her. 'But, the thing is,' she continued, 'he was telling me Helen Mavor's mother was in a right state, the day! The pall bearers could hardly get her off the coffin. They thought she would never allow them to take it out of the house!'

'I can understand *that*,' Kate Emslie said. 'I can *well* understand it.'

Her mother's emphatic confession, surprised Isabel. She would hold me back from *death*, Isabel realised, with dawning wonder. For her mother had never kissed her. Not within her memory. 'That's a *good* Beldie!' she would sometimes say, when she was pleased, or '*Fine* lad, Davie!' But the most tangible expression of her affection was a hurried pat in passing. A trait Isabel had acquired from her. A poor and furtive symbol of things deeply felt. Sometimes, an impulse to kiss Davy overcame Isabel. She would grasp him round the neck, and take him by surprise. '*That's* how Chris B. kisses you, isn't it Davy?' she'd tease him. Pretending it was a kiss from Chris B. And not from herself, at all. It had taken only a kiss to waken Sleeping Beauty up after a hundred years. Isabel's mother might never kiss her into life. But she would hold her back from death itself!

HOLY MOSES!
I am dying

'God, Beldie!' her father's voice warned. 'You nearly had me flat on my face, there! Can you not look where you're going!'

'She takes daft turns like that, whiles,' Davy sniggered. 'Racing about like a mad thing.'

'Beldie!' her father's voice reached her at the byre door. 'What was that gossiping bitch Lil Eadie seeking? She's just taken herself out by the back door!'

Just a Word
Before I go
Bury ME
In silk and satins

The lamp had just been lit in the kitchen. It threw a sudden patch of light across the garden.

I am a stranger. Isabel gathered together the threads of an old, and favourite game. I have lost my way. The wind is beginning to rise. Soon it will be dark. And I must find a bed for the night. *That* looks a friendly house. Any minute now, any minute now, she would race all the way from the byre, and burst into the kitchen, in anticipation of the light and warmth that would rush towards her. And the sound of known voices that would envelop her in their safety.

'Shut that door behind you, Beldie!' her mother warned. 'There's an edge to the nights, now. We don't want to perish!'

But then, Isabel realised, focusing on her family, rooted in their familiar places, they were not strangers. Come in out of the night. They couldn't know how brightly the lamp gleamed. Nor how fiercely the fire burned. They could never catch the cadences of comfort after that wordless lament of the wind along the telegraph wires.

'What was that gossiping bitch Lil Eadie seeking then?' Her father asked.

'O nothing very much,' her mother said, knowing it was just one of the casual observations that gathered the day to an end, and drew in the night. 'She was just on about the funeral. And, speaking about the funeral, was there a big turn out there, the day?'

'Big Bill Mackie was there!' Isabel remembered. 'Lil Eadie said.' She urged the topic on, in the safety of the kitchen. For her mind had skirted round the funeral all day. Approaching it fearfully. Touching it lightly. Retreating from it swiftly, lest it should

capture herself within the isolated circle that contained it. Petri-
fying her in its granite memorial.

'A fair turnout,' her father admitted. 'Considering the fine
harvest weather.' *His* mind walking through the safety of his fields
at Slack-o-Linn. 'George Kerr was saying he's got all his crop,
home. But then,' her father reflected, his fields lie on the sheltered
side of Ben Achie. The hill keeps the sun off mine.'

'Surely!' her mother contradicted. 'The sun must get round to
your fields, *whiles*, Father! *It's* no respecter of persons!'

It seemed another time since Isabel had lain with Else among
the gorse in the Loch Wood, sheltered from the sun. Yet it was
only today. Fear no more the heat o' the sun, she had remembered,
as they scrambled for a hiding place in the shade. How her mind
had been trapped, whirling in search of the rest of the words, that
had eluded it until she found some of her own. Nor its embroiling
ray. The sun, she knew, in a moment of small, distinct, living
clarity, would never reach its zenith, in time and place again,
without the bitter burning smell of gorse.

'I suppose Alick Mearns was at the funeral, the day?' Her
mother was saying. 'All togged up, as usual?'

'Somebody's making their way, here!' Davy announced, flinging his burden of logs down on the hearth. 'I saw the light of a bike
turning down our road.'

'Who can it be at this hour of night?' Kate Emslie's dislike of
unbidden guests found curious outlet in hasty resentful prepar-
ation for them.

'Draw your long legs in about to yourself, Davy. Other folk
would like a glimpse of the fire! And you can just put on your
wellingtons again, Father! Lolling about in your sweaty socks. As
for you, Beldie! Sitting cocked on top of the fire, there. Small
wonder you're always complaining about your chilblains. It's
high time *you* was making tracks for your bed!'

Her commands flew thick and fast. Directed at all. And galvan-
ising each into life.

'It's been a long day,' she reflected, by way of apology, surveying her family sitting upright in formal discomfort. 'A long day for
all of us. You too Beldie,' she added, with dawning remembrance.
'Your last day at school. That must have been some day for you!'

And everybody had forgotten about it. Isabel was curiously
grateful for the world's forgetfulness. One finger probed through
the tenuous fabric of the day and it would disintegrate completely.
For it was not yet shaped and concrete in her mind. Liquid and
elusive, it trickled through her fingers the way the rain from the
roan pipe always eluded capture on its way down to the water
butt.

'Did they all give you your "Bumps" the day, then, Beldie?'
Father asked, jovial, as if the answer really mattered to him.

'I suppose,' her mother ventured, 'that the dominie had a last
word with you. Told you to behave yourself, did he! And work
your work in the world well?'

'Aye,' father remembered. 'When the dominie had his last word
with you, you would have thought you were going away to the
end of the earth! For all that most of us never ventured more than
a mile or two away from the school in our lives.'

'But the *dominie's* time with us had ended,' Kate Emslie
pointed out. 'And that was what counted with him!'

'They FORGOT!' Davy said suddenly, triumphantly, getting
his own back. 'They all got off early for the funeral. And they
forgot all about her last day. Serves her right!'

The loud knock at the back door sent Kate Emslie scurrying to
peer out of the scullery window.

'We are not bedded yet.' The wariness of her greeting reached
them in the kitchen. 'But we are just thinking about it,' she
prophesied ominously.

'It's yourself, is it, Alex?' Father shouted genially forestalling
his wife's reluctance. 'Come away in. Come on in and sit yourself
down man!'

Her blood stirred in recognition. The thousand anonymous

horsemen Isabel had longed to lie under in the dark hay-lofts began to merge into, and take on the identity of the guest by the fire from the gleam of his leggings to the hairs curling red on his hands. And memory completed the picture for her. Until the death of Helen Mavor had ousted him, Alex Ewan had been the object of eternal curiosity and speculation. It was high time he took a wife, some said. He had no need for one, others remembered. You never bought the cow when you got the milk for nothing. And the way the young girls were so willing to open their legs to him he could have fathered the population all on his own. Her mother's bitter denunciation rose to mind.

'Poor bits of lassies, just! *That's* who Alex Ewan takes for his housekeepers. Out of the workhouse with their unfathered bairns. Thankful to take on any job at all to get out of the workhouse. And himself just ready to father another bairn on them! Striding about yonder. Togged up to the nines, always!'

'He's a man that takes a proper pride in himself!' Her father had always defended. 'As well he might. For he's a fine set-up man.'

. . . The Wild Man Of Borneo who had threatened all of childhood's misdemeanours. Feared, but fascinating. Unseen, but always imminent. The word becoming flesh.

'I see they're after going and cancelling the Harvest Home dance,' he was saying. 'Owing to the funeral, I suppose.'

The criticism in his voice stung Kate Emslie into remembered resentment. 'And rightly so!' she snapped. 'It would be a sore pity if the living couldn't catch its breath to have a thought for the dead.'

'That doesn't bring them back, mistress,' Alex Ewan pointed out.

'No! But it shows some respect!'

As usual, Isabel rememberred, her mother had got the last word. Alpha and Omega. As the minister always prophesied threateningly when he snapped the big bible shut. 'The Beginning and the End!'

'In *my* opinion,' her mother's tone left no room for the opinions of others, 'half the trouble in the parish starts off with those dances. Poor Helen Mavor, herself, started her dancing days too young. Too soon.'

That was the thing that was worth dying for! Isabel had discovered it at last. If I could go once. Just *once* to a dance. I'd never ask for another thing in all my life again. That would be enough for me . . . They wore dresses of blue and pink and green. They shimmered in the light, and trailed on the floor. Their shoes were silver.

'And they are beautiful! I've seen them!' she heard herself announcing suddenly. 'In the Milne Hall. On my way home from the Bible class,' she explained, aware of the stiffening up of the kitchen.

'So that's why you're always so late home from the Bible class on a Friday night,' her father reflected. 'I always wondered about that!'

'Everybody *else* goes to the dancing!' she defended. 'Except *me*! I've always got to go to the Bible class.'

'Poor minister.' Her father condoled. 'He must have a very small Bible class, then. Just yourself, is it Beldie?'

'Anyhow! I can please myself where I go after next week!' The insolence that came rarely to Isabel was torn from her now as a protection against ridicule. And instantly regretted . . . *You* can just go straight up to your bed! . . . her mother would command. And the night that had been proud and expanding, with its portents of approaching womanhood, would humble and close over a small girl sent to bed in disgrace.

'Next week is another matter,' her mother said casually, surprisingly evading such a catastrophe. 'What *does* matter, Beldie,' she emphasised, in the way she sometimes did, when they were alone together, 'is that a thing is either true or it's a lie. And whiles, Beldie, whiles,' she paused, speculative and puzzled, '*you* are very guilty of getting them mixed up, I know *this* much! You never set foot in the Milne Hall in your life! It's just not in your nature to push yourself.'

But she *had* heard the music of the dancing. Sounding through the quiet village, following her all the way to Corbie's Wood, and echoing through her mind long after she had reached home. Dispelling sleep itself.

> And you shall drink freely
> The dews of Glensheerlie
> That stream in the starlight
> When Kings dinna ken
> And deep be your meed
> Of the wine that is red

One day. Some day. *She* would dance to the music. She had never danced with a partner. But she had often danced by herself. A dance in which movement was never confined to setts and reels and ritual patterns, but to the interpretation of the moods of a moment. The 'dews of Glensheerlie' had not got the monopoly. She, herself, could . . . 'stream in the starlight' . . . When Kings dinna ken. How she would dance when the time came. How motionless the other dancers would be, mesmerised into immobility by the grace and sweep of her movements . . .

> On either side the river lie
> Long fields of barley and of rye

On and on. Round and round. Till she dropped exhausted from dancing. And the lament rising up around her, loud enough to assail her into consciousness again.

> Dear God! she hath a lovely face

'I said we're losing you, Isabel!' Alex Ewan was saying. 'They tell me you're going away to service in the town.'

'Aye,' her father agreed. 'We are that! Her mother's kind of anxious about it though. Her going so far away from home, like.'

'We've all got to stretch our wings,' Alex Ewan said. 'Some time or other. She'll be fine, though,' he assured them jovially. 'Isabel will be just fine! Won't you, lass? I warrant *you'll* set all the lads by the ears when you get to the town. With a bonnie head of hair on you like that!'

It had always needeed the recognition of others to confirm her own secret potentials. Like the 'trim ankles' her mother had bestowed upon her. Now she had been bequeathed a 'bonnie head of hair'. She could have sung aloud for such emerging talismans. Protections against the Wild Man Of Borneo. Growing spells to cast over a fine set-up man with shining leggings and hairs that glinted red on his hands.

'It is to be *hoped*,' her mother said, 'that Isabel will keep her mind on her *work*! And have more sense than bother herself about the lads in the town!'

'You cannot put old heads on young shoulders, mistress,' Alex Ewan advised, as he rose to go, aware that he had outstayed his cool welcome. It was when he reached the door that he remembered the purpose of his visit.

'That cow of mine has gone clean dry,' he explained. 'She's just at the drop of calving. I was wondering if you might manage to hold me in milk, for the next day or so. And I'll see till't, mistress,' he promised, 'that you'll get her first yield after calving, to make yourself a fine bit of calfie's cheese.'

'We're not all that partial to calfie's cheese.' Kate Emslie rejected the offer. 'We prefer a bit of plain Crowdie.'

'*Surely*, Alex!' Her father lurched up out of his chair. The geniality in his voice consoled Isabel, and atoned for her mother's rudeness. 'Surely we'll hold you in milk! I'll walk you as far as the end of the road. And I'll send Isabel over to your place,' he promised. 'First thing in the morning.'

Davy and her father were already at work. She could hear the reaper whirring across the Low Field. Her father perched on top of it, disembodied in the rising mist, as he skimmed along the edges of the uncut corn. Davy bobbing up and down behind him gathering the swathes as they fell.

'A thin crop the year,' her father had grumbled. 'More thistles than corn.' As the day warmed, and the pace quickened, Davy would grow careless, grasping wildly at the swathes till his hands 'stooned' all over with thistle stobs. Thistle down puffed along on the breeze would get into his eyes and soon he would start to pray for the reaper to break down. Just for a minute. Just to let him get his back straightened. It was the greatest blessing in all the world, Isabel realised, straightening herself up at the window, not to have a 'crick' in your back.

Down in the hens'ree the Rhode Island Reds clamoured greedily around her mother's feet. 'Hens always died in debt,' her mother would grumble in one breath, confessing in the next that she would be 'fair lost without them.'

The limitations that landmarked her mother's life increased Isabel's growing sense of freedom. When the red flowering currant, barren in its old age, hadn't come into bloom her mother's lament had echoed its regret all through the spring. 'I should have taken a cutting or two when that bush was young. I just never seemed to get the time.' Mourning was contagious, though. The bush, that could no longer flower, had forced itself into leaf. Crumbling the leaves between her fingers, and sniffing them, casually, absentmindedly, one day, with no thought of grief, the limitations had closed in on Isabel too. Spring would never be spring until the flowering currant came into bloom.

'Get a move on, Beldie!' her mother shouted up at the window. 'You should have been on your road with Alex Ewan's milk long since!'

Far into the night, she had heard her mother nagging away at her father. 'Whatever possessed you to suggest that *Beldie* should go *near* Alex Ewan's place!' had been her refrain. 'You know *fine* what that man is!'

'Who else could I send, but Beldie?' her father had defended. 'I can't spare *Davy*! We're making a start to the Low Field. First thing in the morning. Me and Davy!'

Davy would always be captive, within the landmarks. Isabel's pity for him was tinged with some vague sense of regret for herself. Her excitement over her own unknown future, diminished a little by a reluctant envy of Davy's safety in the familiar.

> . . . we ken a Place
> where the trout leaps *great*
> me – and Davy

Always, Isabel felt an intruder in the kitchen in the early mornings. Cool and dim and aloof, it seemed to hold itself in reserve for the heat and busyness of her *mother's* day. The stone flags her mother had just scrubbed were still damp to the touch of Isabel's bare feet. Their high wet shine had not yet dried up into sand streaked greyness.

'*You* slept your head into train oil, this morning!' her mother grumbled, clattering down the hens' pail and shattering the silence of the kitchen. 'You've got a long travel in front of you!' she reminded. 'Alex Ewan's place is away at the back of beyond!'

'I was brushing my hair,' Isabel said. Suddenly remembering the thought that leapt up in her mind on wakening . . . He said I'd bonnie hair . . .

'You have more need to get something on your *feet*!' her mother advised. 'Padding about the damp floor! You may have *brushed* your hair,' her mother added, surveying Isabel dubiously, 'But I see you haven't tied it *back*! You know fine how I feel about your hair flying all round your face!'

'Else Finlay has *ringlets*!' Isabel remembered. '*Her* mother puts them in for Else, every night. With papers!'

'More fool her *mother*! That's all *I* can say!' Kate Emslie banged the hens' pail down on the kitchen floor. And silenced the counsel for the defence.

But *she* had 'bonnie hair'. The knowing sang in Isabel's mind all the way down Slack-o-Linn road. At the end of it, the world widened, and the day began to widen with it, in growing confliction. This time next week she would be walking along a new road. Through a strange country. Landmarks that were rooted in her first consciousness became distorted. She had the curious feeling that she walked suspended through a world at once timeless and unreal. Poised on the stile that led into Corbie's Wood, she stirred herself, and thought. Yesterday, when I crossed this stile, I was on my way to School. I'll never cross the stile to go *that* way, again.

'*You're* out of your road this morning, Isabel!' the wives waiting for the bus greeted her, when she got to the crossroads. 'Surely you should be giving your mother a hand on a Saturday!'

'I'm away over to Alex Ewan's place with some milk,' she told them. 'His cow has gone clean dry!'

'*Himself* hasn't!' the joiner's wife said drily.

'More's the pity!' Lil Eadie agreed.

'You want to watch yourself with that one!' they all advised. 'It's a while since he's had one young enough to have all her own teeth.'

Their laughter rose in spasms around her.

'Time, somebody gave him a damned good bite!' the joiner's wife egged their laughter on.

Time Isabel was away to service in the town. Away from the coarseness that lurked around the bus stop, ready to spring up, and trap her in embarrassment.

Time to be glad her mother was her mother! For *she* would never stand skirling daft, at the cross roads. Would never never kilt her skirt high above her knees, as Lil Eadie was doing now. Prancing around, exhorting the other wives to admire her 'Long John Toms'. Her 'passion killers'.

Time coming soon, now, when Isabel would escape from all! Dark and mysterious she would be, the next time she passed that lot! 'Good afternoon,' she would say. Cool. Without pausing. Taking her dark, mysterious self past the bus stop, intact.

'Surely that was *Kate Emslie's* lass!' they would speculate, mystified, when she passed them.

'Her that went away to service in the town!'

The village before her lay misted and relaxed under its Saturday morning idleness. The women, their cottages 'thoroughed out' before they went to bed on Friday night, stood at their ease on their cardinal red doorsteps calling across to each other without urgency. The way the wood pigeons had cooed and coodled all the length of Corbie's Wood. And just as the crackle of a twig had silenced the wood pigeons, so the hen man's van, roaring its way through the village, now silenced the women into critical contemplation of the dust it raised up behind it.

Walking in the wake of the van, Isabel was aware of the attention instantly transferred on herself. She was too old now to escape it by kicking out at any stone that barred her way and scudding defiantly past the watchful wives.

'That hen van's a perfect menace,' the shoemaker's wife informed the others.

'One of these fine *days*!' the beadle's wife prophesied.

'So *you've* come to see the flowers too, then, Isabel!'

They swirled round on her, as if they had spotted her in unison with those eyes they always claimed they had in the back of their heads.

'All that *way* from Slack-o-Linn!'

'Mind *you*! They're well worth seeing!' Teen Ross assured them from her stance by the pump. 'There's a small *fortune* on that grave. And *no* mistake!'

'I don't hold with it, for all *that*!' the shoemaker's wife said. 'I'm one who likes flowers well enough to let them grow!' she boasted, hemmed neatly in by her hedge of boxwood. Spiked and enclosed by all her zinnias. The loss of *one* would have outflanked her.

'Come and see the flowers, Isabel,' Else Finlay invited when she reached the kirk gate.

'They're all white!' Jean Mavor said.

'White everywhere!' her sister agreed.

'Come on, Isabel!' Else urged, aware of her hestitation, for a barrier, subtle, but stronger than the kirk gate had arisen to separate Isabel from Else, and all her erstwhile classmates, kneeling on the grass, examining the cards on the high bank of wreaths. Although she had left school only yesterday, it was long enough to exile her from their inner circle.

'Have you lot read *this* one?' Ann Mavor demanded. '"Safe On His Gentle Breast",' she interpreted in a reading-aloud voice. '"With Love Always. Mimmy".'

'Mimmy was Helen Mavor's grandmother,' Isabel said. And the barrier became tangible, as the others rose up off their knees and dumbly appraised her from the other side of the gate.

'It's an old Scottish word for grandmother.' She rushed into, and through the silence.

'We all know *that*!' Jean Mavor said.

'We know that, fine!' her sister echoed.

'*Anyhow*!' Isabel shrugged, for the moment had come to turn and go. 'Anyhow. I haven't got *time* to see the flowers. I've got to go over to Alex Ewan's place,' she added, infusing her mission with distance and importance. 'He's got to get milk. His cow's gone dry.'

No statement, she discovered to her own surprise, could have so effectively and firmly established her growing adult awareness.

'Alex EWAN's place!' they chorused, crowding round the gate, admiringly and apprehensively.

'*He's* just sent his latest housekeeper down the road!' Else confided. 'Sacked her on the spot. Our servant met her at the bus stop. Pram. Bairn. And all!'

'He'll be all by *himself*, then, Isabel!' Jean Mavor warned. 'Are you not feared to go there on your *own*?'

'Not . . . feared,' she admitted at last. And in the wake of her considered admission, realisation overtook her. She *wanted* to go. She wanted to go, more than anything else in all the world. '*Never* feared!' She threw back her head and laughed at the bewildered expressions on their faces. And for the relief of a truth acknowledged.

'Come on in, Isabel. Come on and see the flowers,' Else urged, and holding the gate open, stepped aside to let a grown-up acquaintance enter through.

She could never have gone to see the flowers. She knew that with every step that led her away from the kirkyard. She would have wanted to toss away the flowers. To see beneath and beyond them. To claw through the grave with her bare hands and penetrate the mystery of death itself.

O, she knew well enough what happened to the *ancient* dead. When the small graveyard was full the gravedigger just dug up some of the old graves and shovelled the contents over the dyke to make room for the newcomers. And that seemed fair enough. For they were old. Older than anybody's memory of them. As remote and far sounding as the inscriptions that struggled brokenly through the moss, encrusted on their slanting tombstones . . . Until the Day Breaks and the Shadows Flee Away.

Five, short days ago Helen Mavor had been alive.

'Here today. Gone tomorrow,' her mother remarked, as she washed the eggs. Counting them in the same breath. Certain that *she* would be there to sell them to the hen man tomorrow.

We'll all go to our long home *some* day. The congregation had reminded each other, as they clustered round the kirk gate after the memorial service. Casually, as if there was no hurry at all for *them* to go to *their* long home.

That bourne from which no traveller ever returns. The minister had forecast, with gloomy conviction. That had *not* convinced Isabel.

Lay hold on
LIFE
And it
Shall BE
Thy joy and Crown

Ee
ter
NALLY

How often had they sang that in the kirk. And how she had hugged its sentiment to herself, in an embrace wide enough to hold the years to come and all that they might bring. And the years that had gone and all that they had brought.

Helen Mavor could never have let go of life so soon. Could never be as dead as that so suddenly. Lying under her bank of white flowers so near to the kirk door, memory must surely still hold good! She would know when it was spring.

They would all be singing.

There is a green hill far away
Without a city wall

And summer. She would remember it when they sang

For the beauty of the earth
For the beauty of the skies
For the love which from our birth

And autumn. She would remember it, too, from the nearby singing sounds

Earth seems to squander her plenty on the sheaf

But Helen Mavor had at least seen a bit of this autumn, she remembered, gazing across the landscape. The thought halted her and fixed her to the spot. I'm seeing it for Helen, she realised.

Watchful. Expectant of some subtle change. From now on, she promised, I'll look at things for her. She won't miss so much, that way.

Clambering over the dyke, she raced down Teuchat's Hill towards the river. The rattle of her milk can scattering the grazing ewes and their half grown lambs. There had been no 'lambie's storm' in the spring, to her father's relief, so it was some of his lambs that stared after her, scandalised, from beneath the fleecy safety of their mothers' flanks.

'You're *our* lambs!' she shouted back, reminding them. 'So you can put *that* in your pipes and smoke it!'

'You'd better go by the road,' her mother had advised, when she set out in the morning. 'For, if you take the short cut by the river, knowing *you* you'll just plooter about there, all day!'

But she hadn't plootered about the river. And there were some things her mother didn't know about her. She could leave things behind fine! It was just that things would never let her go! And so the river ran on behind her, tugging away at mind and memory. The dark murky hiding places of the tiddlers in the deep water at its edge. The forget-me-nots that skimmed along its banks, rooted down in the water itself.

Frail life-lines you'd clutch at laughingly, to land. The stones that rose at random to form their own peculiar pattern for stepping over. The wild raspberries, their brief enticement broken by a more potent siren sound.

'Last across the stepping stones is a *hairy worm*!'

The roofs of the Smiddy Crofts swayed redly towards her through the blue haze. 'Half way to the back of beyond,' her mother described the Crofts. 'And we'll get there by and by.' The shadows of the trees began to lattice the road into great squares of sunlight.

Iggledy Piggledy
ONE!
TWO!
THREE!
I love my
LOVE
And my Love
Loves
ME!!

'They must have money to burn on shoe leather at Slack-o-Linn!'

The unbeliever's wife stood in the dimness, half folded over the gate of her cottage.

'I've got a stone in my shoe.' She hopped to a halt, reddening under her instant lie.

'A queer way to get rid of a stone in your shoe.' The unbeliever's wife looked over and past her to the wood beyond. 'Leaping about the road like that!'

But then, the unbeliever's wife knew nothing about stones in shoes, she re-assured herself, remembering to hirple lamely till she was out of sight. There was luxury in the pain of a stone in your shoe. And a feeling of power. You could end it instantly. Or endure it forever. The longer you held on to the pain, the sweeter the ease. She would never know such ease, the unbeliever's wife, for she would never endure such agony.

'The fear of the Lord is the beginning of wisdom,' her mother always quoted, when there was an argument at home over the unbeliever.

'He's a brave man. For all that he doesn't hold with the kirk,' her father would insist. 'Awarded medals to prove it! Not that he took them, mind you! For he's a man who knows his own mind. A man that went all through the blood bath of the Somme.'

Her father's highly coloured, far sounding vindications of the unbeliever never narrowed down to match the reality of the small, whey-faced man himself. As shadowy and withdrawn as his cottage that huddled amongst the trees. When Isabel came across him at all, it was accidental, with the wordlessness of unexpected impact. If words could have been uttered, they would have been words of apology for some inexplicable intrusion.

The unbeliever only came to life in her mind on Armistice Sundays. And then by his absence. When medals for bravery glinted and jingled on other men's breasts. And his voice never rose to swell the triumphant volume of

> When Zion's bondage God turned back
> As men that dreamed were *we*
> Then filled with laughter were our souls
> Our tongues with melody

'Where's the fire, then, Isabel?' The blacksmith's apprentice grinned from the door of the forge. 'You're fair out of puff.'

'That's because I ran all the way from the river with Alex Ewan's milk.'

'It'll be into butter by now, then!'

'Or buttermilk!' she suggested, as they laughed at the ridiculous idea, pleased with each other's wit. She hadn't laughed so much for such a long time, over such a little thing.

'I could swing this milk can right round my head. And I wouldn't spill a drop,' she claimed, nudging the tears of laughter from her cheeks.

'I bet you could too!' the blacksmith's apprentice said. 'It's the speed that does it,' he explained. 'It doesn't give the milk time to fall out.'

'Is *that* what it is?' she asked, her attention straying to the hair on his chest. Matted with sweat, it streaked down to his navel in a long black line.

A hairy man's a happy man, her father always said, lathering himself above the sink. But a hairy wife's a witch! Yet, it was important for a woman to be hairy, according to Else.

'I'll show you if you show me!' Else had once challenged. She hadn't accepted the challenge. Else only ever dared anything, when she was sure she would win.

She wouldn't let herself look at *his* navel, either! 'Belly button' her mother called it, that shut you in and held you together. You'd just pop out and spill all over, if it wasn't there.

'A shame the dance was cancelled on Friday,' the blacksmith's apprentice said, as if it was a regret they both should share.

'Wasn't it just!' The brightness that flashed up inside her sharpened her voice. She could feel it flooding her face and thrusting itself out from behind her eyes. That was what her hair loose, and her Sunday shoes did for her! She always knew they'd do that. Make her worthy enough to go to a dance. Even if she would never have been allowed to go in the first place!

'Maybe it will be on next Friday, though,' he suggested.

'Maybe.'

'Maybe we'll see you there, then?'

'Maybe.'

'Next Friday then!'

'Next Friday!' she confirmed, shouting back, as she ran forward in some bright, expectant certainty.

If she'd had whooping cough it would have been cured the instant she turned round into the Lecht Road. The fumes rose hotly from its newly tarred surface. Best cure in the world for whooping cough, her mother always said. In the days when folk had big families and no money to throw away on doctors. She'd never tried it herself, mind you! But she'd heard tell of many an infant snatched from death's door by a sniff of the tar. Nonsense! Her father had contared. For he had no faith in miracles. Pure nonsense just! You went when your time came. Tar or no tar.

It was the kind of road that lured her into navigating it blind. When all sense of direction lay in the sensitivity of her feet. Veering sideways across the softness of the grass verge, teetering cautiously over the gritty gravel, shoe bound at last on the soft sticky tar.

'A menace to other folk. As well as to yourself!' Postie shouted. His bike grinding to a halt on the gravel. 'It's a blind corner that. And bloody dangerous!'

But then, she was a blind person! Though Postie would never believe that, she realised, staring startled up at him.

'I could have gone arse over heels!' he claimed. 'With you stuck on the road. Like a damned idiot!'

There was something odd about Postie, himself, she remembered. Searching his face to find it.

'You'll surely know me the next time you see me!' he snarled, remounting his bike. 'Stupid little bitch! You haven't even got the sense you was born with.'

Her mother had never been able to put her finger on what was odd about Postie. Though any man on the wrong side of forty with a secure job like his and a fine pension at the end of it, still stuck to his mother's apron strings must be an odd bod, right enough!

Not everybody was in such a rush to get the marriage banns cried out in the kirk as she herself had been, Father had always defended. *Some* folk likit to hold to their bit of freedom. Though few enough got the chance to do it. Poor buggers!

Maybe so. Her mother had snapped. But it always took two! And there was no call for language! Though *some* mothers had a lot to account for! If it was Davy now! She, herself, would only be too pleased to see *him* settled down with a nice sensible lass.

'If it was *me*,' Davy had boasted, perking up under the unexpected attention, 'and I had *Postie's* mother, I'd take the King's Shilling!'

Wondrous shilling. Splendid shilling. Sounding always as if it was an honour conferred upon His Majesty. Sire, I will *accept* your shilling. Silver talisman that opened for Davy all avenues of escape. Gaining currency and glimmer on dark frostbitten mornings in winter, when she'd pass Davy on her road to school, howking turnips out of the stone hard earth in the Low Park. Hardly a copper to call his own, he'd confide, whacking his arms across his chest to get the blood going in his fingers again. His bed and his bite, just. And a bare bob or two in his pocket to tide him over a Friday night. For pure slavery. He'd be far better off with the King's Shilling. Other things he'd confide too, on such mornings. Things only half comprehended, as she stood absorbed in her breath, that abstract thing they said you could die for the want of, becoming tangible at last, rising white in the darkness. He'd hardly get anybody *better* than Chris B. Her not being all that particular. And, God knows, he didn't want the likes of *her*! Not with the one suit he'd had for three years. And it away above his ankles now. Near enough to make him a laughing-stock in the countryside. Though she didn't care! Not listening to a word he was telling her!

'But Mother,' she had remembered, keeping her eyes fixed on the breath that was drifting away from her, 'gets the Co-op van. Even if it *is* dearer than the other vans. Just so that she can get our clothes off the Divi. It's the only way she can save.'

'How many pounds of sugar do you think it takes, Beldie, to get enough Divis for one serge suit?' Davy had asked, in the voice the dominie always used when he knew she would never find the answer. Never. In a million years.

If a tank containing eighty-five gallons of water leaked at the rate of . . .

At least, she didn't have to worry herself about tanks that leaked any more. And for Davy there was always the King's Shilling.

Yet not, not in *all* its glory, did the King's Shilling have the high allure of that *other* enlistment fee her mother sometimes sang of, bent over the washing-board in the tub, on high wind-blown mornings.

For my lad
Would list
When the Duchess
Kissed
He forgot
All the vows
He made
He turned
And he took
But one last long
Look
When
'The Cock O' the North'
Was
Played

The hard surface of Leuchar's Road rang out under her feet. How Alan Soutar would have struck the blue sparks out of the stones, on a road like this, with the heel-rings of his boots! She had never mastered the knack. It was the twist of the heel that did it, he'd always boasted. Making a fine thing out of it. Not that she had cared. He could only make the sparks, it was herself, racing on behind him, who saw them all rising up.

He forgot
All the vows
He made
He turned
And he took
But one last long
Look

'Sing in the morning. Cry before night,' the Howdie Wife prophesied, peering above her byre door.

'Isabel, is it?' Shading her eyes against the sun, she began to piece her together, bit by bit. 'Isabel, surely! Isabel. Isabel Emslie! Though you'll not be minding on *me*!' The old woman thrust her face forward, anxious for recognition.

The Howdie Wife everybody called her. Everybody except Isabel's mother. Anybody. She said. Who brought you naked into the world. And spruced you up to go out of it, deserved the respect of their proper name. For they were in at the beginning of life. And at its end. And that, surely, was a something!

The first person to set eyes on her. Isabel tried to infuse the thought with awe. Stark naked at that! Her body felt no embarrassment, having outgrown the Howdie Wife's memory. The first person to touch her. The old woman's hands, scratching away at the nape of her neck, had outgrown that memory too. Hard to tell whether the old woman approved of her handiwork, hard to get out from, or under, that silent appraisal.

'Rob Emslie will never die! As long as *you* live. You carry him in your face!'

Triumph rang out of the old woman's voice. 'You're small bookit, though,' she considered critically. 'Like your mother. But fleet of foot like herself. Fleet of foot.'

The sudden flash of memory increased the old woman in stature, and stabbed Isabel with envy.

Tell me. Tell me again. Tell me about the days when *you* was young.

How insistently she had deaved her mother for the stories of *her* young days. Stories that were never allowed to deviate in detail. To add to themselves. Or to take away. So that the young girl who became her mother ran forever through cone strewn fir woods, clothed eternally in a grey frock with blue braiding at the neck, a blue calico pinny with two pockets and black boots that buttoned right up to her knees. She always felt very close to that young girl. As if they could have been friends together. Best friends. The way herself and Else was. Sometimes, she ran ghost-like through the fir woods of her mother's stories, singing along with her.

> Poor old Robinson Crusoe
> I wonder how he could do so!
> He made him a coat
> Of an old nanny goat
> Poor old Robinson Crusoe

'The thing is.' The Howdie Wife thrust her face forward, till it almost touched her own. 'The thing is. She could never give you the breast.'

'I've got to go, Mistress Mutch. I've got to be back before dinner-time.'

'Either *that*!' The Howdie Wife said. 'Or her milk didn't lie on your stomach.'

'I've got to go, Mistress Mutch.' Instantly. Urgently out of the cone strewn fire woods of memory, before the ghostly girls who sang their way through them took on the burdens of their flesh.

'I'm TELLING you!'

The old woman's voice halted her in her tracks. 'There was only one cow the country round whose milk you'd suckle. Only *one*. The wee blue at Broadbec Inn. A wild Inn, yon. Still is on a Friday night. Still is. Oh, I could tell you a thing or two.'

Withdrawing her face, the old woman withdrew the things she could tell. Holding them all to herself, in the far away reflection of her eyes. Isabel knew the look. She'd sometimes seen it on her mother's face. Staring out of the window, yet not seeing what was beyond it. She never told what she had seen either!

'A wild Inn I was saying.'

The old woman's voice rose shrill behind her. Desperate at having let her captive audience go.

'A wild Inn. And WANTON!'

The white gates at the level crossing snapped shut to let the train go by. Its warning bell rang high up in the signal box. But they could sometimes hear the train coming long before the bell told of it. Herself and Else. Flinging themselves down on the grassy embankment, listening with their ears against the ground. Giggling together at the helpless anger of the signal man, shaking his fist at his high window. Racing like the wind the moment the train passed and set the signal man free. Racing against the train itself to reach the bridge before it thundered beneath it. Standing high and bereft on the bridge, holding on to the train till the last wisp of steam curling round and below, disappeared at Ben Achie.

Further down the line, Postie trundled his bike across the sleepers, raising his hand to the signal man in acknowledgement of such a privilege. He never allowed anybody else to break the rules, did Postie. Wouldn't take an unstamped letter from her mother. Not even with the tuppence to buy the stamp. 'Against government rules, Mistress Emslie,' he'd insist. 'More than my job's worth!' A man who wouldn't even give you the dirt from between his toes, her father always said. Though why anyone should ever want that puzzled Isabel. And there he was, breaking the rules himself, taking the short cut that would have taken a mile off her own journey. It might be good to be old. You could break all the rules then. She, herself, might have taken the risk, if the signal man's eye wasn't fixed upon her. She might *still* have taken it if Else had been there to run it with her. Laughing in the wind, and in the face of the signal man. She missed Else.

LNER. The yellow letters flashed out and by on the green engine. And the train took on a personal identity. *Her* train. The train she herself would be sitting in on Monday morning. She'd watch out for the signal box. And for the bridge. She might even wave to the signal man, grinning at her right to do so. She'd remember Else. And maybe, maybe she'd find out at last if the steam really *did* disappear forever, when the train went round and under Ben Achie.

From *this* side of the bridge Ben Achie should have been transformed. Should have put on another face and laughed and rejoiced, the way the psalms and the paraphrases urged in the kirk on Sunday mornings.

It should have lifted up its voice and sung in the accents of all the people who lived and worked below it, who had died in its shadow, who had never even set eyes on it. For this was the 'back' of Ben Achie. Landmarked in the imagination, rooted in nostalgic memory. Pondering in the shimmering heat, it looked as if it might just make up its mind to rise up and do all, or any of those things, till the eye settled on the stocks circled beneath it. Only the men turning the stocks had motion. Only the dogs worrying at them, had voice.

'A penny for them, Isabel.' Alick Mearns grinned across at her, from the other side of the fence.

'Would tuppence buy them, maybe?'

She shook her head.

'I canna afford to bid higher,' the crofter sighed. 'Some lad or other?' he suggested.

'It's Ben Achie,' she said. 'I thought it would look different from the back.'

'You did, did you?' Turning to face the hill, the crofter joined in her silent search for the difference.

'Do you know something, Isabel?' he said, sharing the secrecy of his discovery at last. 'There's no back to Ben Achie. No back to it at all. But that's between you and me, of course. Ourselves two. And the both of us! It's like this,' he explained, and she knew from the twinkle in his eyes that he was laughing at her. 'It's like this. When I look at Ben Achie from my Park here, that's the *front* of it for me, but if I was to take a dander over the bridge and across the river to *your* place at Slack-o-Linn, that would be the *back* of it for me! Have you got that *clear*, now?'

'Aye.' She nodded to confirm it. For it seemed important to him that she'd 'got it' clear.

A well doing man, Alick Mearns, was her family's verdict on the crofter. Even if he *was* old and never took a wife, and lived by himself. They never saw anything odd about him. But then, as her father often pointed out, Alick Mearns had never neglected himself. Taking a turn over, every now and again, to see Nell Simmers. To see to her *henhouses*! Her mother would snap, for no apparent reason. Her being a widow woman and all.

Then there was that time in Canada her father sometimes spoke of. Just after the war, when lots of the crofter's sons emigrated, to wait for the deaths of their fathers, to inherit the crofts.

Alick Mearns had been one of them. But he had always leapt long-legged out of anonymity. According to her father, he had chased all over Canada. After a lass. Her father's voice had always held the pride of Marathon, in the telling of it. And Canada, she remembered, had ever after seemed more familiar than all the other far away countries in the geography lessons. Losing all the immensity the dominie lent it, in a small, intimate picture of Alick Mearns chasing all over it. After a lass.

Strange, that the image of him in Canada had more reality than the man stood in front of her had in the flesh.

Coming to kirk only on Communion Sundays. Absolved by her *mother* for his rare attendances. A man on his own with both croft and house to mind. It would be a crying shame if the kirk session deprived him of his Communion token. You'd got to make allowances. The kirk, above all!

An elusive man, Alick Mearns. Hovering dimly on the outskirts of the parish. 'I gave Alick Mearns a wave,' her father would mention when he came home from the Mart. 'Alick Mearns gave me a nod,' he'd remember when he came home from a roup. 'I caught a glimpse of him in the distance.'

A far away man. He gave you a nod. You gave him a wave. Symbols becoming tangible. Kindly things handed out to each other. Across the distances.

'So you *see*, Isabel,' he was urging, 'Nobody can ever rightly say they've seen the *back* o' Ben Achie. But the thing is. The thing is,' he assured her twinkling, 'you and me have seen Ben Achie itself!'

Where the Gadie rins
Where the Gadie rins
O gin I were
Where Gadie rins
At the back
O Ben Achie

I never had
But twa right lads
But twa right lads
But twa right lads
I never had
But twa right lads
At the back
O Ben Achie

And ane was killed
At Louden Fair
At Louden Fair
And ane was killed
At Louden Fair
And the other
Was drowned

This was the first time she had ever been to Alex Ewan's croft. The track that led to it turned off the main road so suddenly that she almost ran on past it. The sign identifying it slanted inwards, as if outsiders were unwelcome, and those who belonged would never lose their way, anyhow.

Red Hill, the signpost claimed. The croft that held the chosen man. The sight of it disappointed her. It lacked the mystery of the furtive whispers at the bus stop and the school playground. It had none of the high gleam and glitter its owner had kindled in her mind's eye. It could have been Slack-o-Linn, her own home, lying grey and low. Half hidden in the tall barley.

The thing about a house without a woman, her mother often said, was just that it lacked a woman's touch. Always emphasising her *own* touch. Holding the jam she had just made admiringly up against the light. Whisking the invisible dust off her highly polished dresser.

'You found your road, then!' He came towards her. Smaller than he had appeared in her vision in the night. Those secretive nights, when, neither asleep nor awake, she'd lie in a world populated only by herself, but wide enough to hold any partner of her choosing. Narrow enough to isolate them both, beneath the darkness of the blankets. Fragile world. Shattered on the instant of her mother's footsteps sounding lightly on the stairs. Not to be rebuilt till her mother shut the bedroom door behind her for the night. Tortuous re-erection. Never to be rushed. Needing such perfection, in such a small thing as a name. Like nights when she rejected the partnership of the tenor in the kirk choir. Alan Soutar. And the young minister who always took over when the old one went to the General Assembly. Nights when she even handed Rochester back to Jane Eyre. And Heathcliff to Catherine Earnshaw. Building up for herself an image of some new, unknown partner. Sometimes falling asleep before she could find the right name for him. For he could never come into existence until he had a name. Often lying awake in an agony of frustration. Because the name wouldn't come.

'Do *you* ever dream, Elsc?' she had once asked. In the hope that she might not be alone in such shameful delight and painful frustration.

'*Do* you, Else?' knowing she would never get the true answer because she hadn't asked the true question.

'Sometimes,' Else had said. 'But my mother says you only dream if you lie on your back.'

She had never dreamed lying on her back.

'I was beginning to think that maybe you'd got lost,' he was saying.

'No.' She shook her head, bending to clap the old moth-eaten collie at his side. Burying her face in the hairy foostiness of the dog's neck.

'He's an old fool!' Alex Ewan said. 'He'll take any amount of that!'

'Our Nell does too! My father says she'll never make a good sheep dog.' She rushed on. Surprised herself, by her sudden volubility. 'Because she's just everybody's dog. He says a good sheep dog has only one master. Nell *will* come to you when you shout "HEEL!" But she just sits looking at you, with her paw up, begging, when you tell her to go "Way WIDE!" My father says she's a young fool!'

'I'll take the can off you,' he said, lifting the sneck of the door. I've got the kettle on the boil. You'll be the better of a cup of tea. After your long travel.'

'I've got to get back!' The urgency of truth rang out in her own ears. 'I haven't got time!'

'Time to hold on, surely, till I empty the can for you!'

'There's no hurry for the milk can,' she assured him. 'Mother said Davy can collect the can at night.' Just you hand it in to Alex Ewan, her mother had insisted. And be on your way, again!

'Oh she *did*, did she?' Alex Ewan clattered the can down on the porch floor. 'But she *would*, of course. I've got something better than a cup of tea for you,' he said, straightening up, and speaking to her again. 'And you'll never guess what it *is*, Isabel! It's the new calfie! Born less than an hour since. I'll wager you've never set eyes on a calfie as newly born as *this* chappie!'

'Just one kiss, Isabel. A wee kiss. *That'll* not harm you.'

Crushed against the cow's stall in the sweating dimness of the byre, with the sharn, sharp and strong rising up and nipping her eyes, and the smell of tobacco on his breath, mingling with her own, the dark haylofts of her heated imagination had become real, at last.

'It's all right, Isabel. It's all right, lass. I'm not going to hurt you.'

Easing her down into the straw and stroking her hair, he whispered its bonnieness into her ears. 'Easy, lass. Easy now. Easy.'

'*Never* feared!' she had boasted to the girls, in a moment of bravado. Only feared now, because her boast was coming true. Feared that he would discover the shamelessness of her urgent need. Rigid and disciplined under the touch of his hand groping under the elastic of her knickers. Terrified lest she should urge him on in tongues. In words unknown. And still unheard of.

O Isabel. Isabel. Pettie. My Pettie.

His hands had lost their tenderness. Urgent and fierce and thrusting . . .

Postie's bell clanging across the yard hustled them to their feet.

'Get that straw out of your hair!' Alex Ewan said, staring at her as if she was somebody he had never set eyes on before. 'And for God's sake, tidy yourself up a bit! Get a *move* on!' he urged, as she stood shamed into immobility. Her knickers dangling below her knees shamed her far more than his hand groping up them in the darkness had done. 'Postie will be on us in a minute.' He warned, flicking his trousers down with his hands, and whistling towards the byre door. Suddenly an ordinary man, shouting an ordinary greeting on an ordinary morning.

'Aye, Postie. Another fine day again, then!'

'It could be worse,' Postie admitted. 'I thought I might find you round here. Has the calf come, then?'

'Only just, Postie. A real fine beastie.'

'You've got company, I see.' Postie halted at the Byre door. 'Isabel. Isabel Emslie.'

'O aye.' Alex Ewan glanced at her, as if he, himself had just become aware that he had company. 'She's just been with my milk. She wanted to see the new calf.'

'A bull calf,' Postie said, peering down into the calf's box.

'Man, Alex! But that'll be *another* subsidy for you. Still.' Postie straightened up to consider it. 'Still. Subsidy or no subsidy, there's a lot to be said for a little heifer! Would you not agree, now, Alex?'

The laughter, rising up around her, seemed to derive itself from her. But did not include her.

'You should make your feet your friends, Isabel!' Alex Ewan advised, when the laughter died down. 'Your mother will be wondering where you've got to all this time!'

Juggling with time. Losing herself in the recollected safety of last Tuesday's silent reading period.

It was the best of times. It was the worst of times. A fair haired queen . . .

Thrusting herself forward into the oblivion of the days that were still to come. Getting down off the stile and walking into and through the days. Proud and elusive. Past the forge where the men all gathered on Friday nights. Past Alex Ewan. Most of *all*, past Alex Ewan. Stockings straight. Hair sleek and shining. Skirt swinging in a high wind blowing. Showing the seductive sheen of *silken* knickers!

A cool miss *that* one's turned into! They'd murmur together, as she passed. The way they spoke of the doctor's daughter, when she came home on holiday from the university.

I wouldn't mind getting her in amongst the whins for five minutes! I'd soon take the fire out of her!

For never. Never again would she stand not knowing what to do. Crumpled and sticky and dirty, with her knickers dangling around her knees. And herself be told to 'tidy up'.

Walking furtively through the field that lay fallow at the back of the house. Time slipping out of her control altogether. Forcing her feet into the almost forgotten habit of side stepping the clusters of the last of the summer's daisies. Shamefulness falling away from her in the intense, absorbed recollection of early praise from morning memory

Daisies are
our *silver*
buttercups our
gold
this is
all
the treasure
we
can *have*
or hold.

'She should have been home long by *this* time!' her mother's voice drifted complainingly out, from the scullery window. 'But she's been on the simmer this past day or two. No settle in her. No settle at all!'

'It's youngness, woman!' – her father was insisting. 'Youngness just. And that's an ill we *all* get cured of. If we live long enough.'

'You took your time!' Her mother swivelled round from the baking board and searched her face for the reason. Davy and her father turning to join her in the search.

'I got lost –'

It surprised herself, that she could look at them. And lie so calmly.

'I'd an awful job finding Alex Ewan's place.'

'Oh that's easily enough done!' her father said, turning round to the fire again, and accepting the lie for them all. 'Yon's the kind of place where you could meet yourself coming back.'

'The new calfie came!' She remembered. Seeing it sudden and clear, as she had never been aware of seeing it in the byre.

'A wee bull calfie a bonnie wee thing it was! It's funny, isn't it? It's got teeth. But it sucks your fingers without hurting them. The way the foster lambs suck.'

'*That*!' her mother said, thumping the rolling pin down on the oat cakes, 'will mean *another* subsidy for Alex Ewan. That man just *lives* on subsidies!'

'I swear to God!' her father chuckled in agreement, 'yon's a man can always pick himself a cow that will only throw bull calves!'

'A heifer's best though,' Isabel remembered. 'They say a heifer's best.'

'A heifer doesn't bring in the ready cash!' her mother pointed out. 'And speaking about cash, Nell Simmers called in by when you was out. She'd just been down to see the flowers on Helen Mavor's grave. Same old Nell! Grumbling away as usual. Said the cost of the flowers on yon grave would have keepit *her* feet shod for a year! But, as I pointed out to her,' her mother's hand paused in its careful division of her oatcakes, as if it was important to consider *precisely* what she had pointed out. 'As I pointed out. If Helen Mavor had gotten the chance she would willingly have given up *all* the flowers on her grave. For sake of running barefoot again.'

> *Buttercups*
> our gold
> *this* is
> *all*
> the treasure
> *we*
> can *have*

Stormy Weather

'You lot gone deaf! First bell's gone!'

Bertha stood at the dormitory door. Cocooned within a subtle 'insolence of office', recently acquired when she had been promoted from being 'one of the orphanage girls' to 'orphanage servant'.

'Lying steaming there!'

'Steaming', uttered in Bertha's voice, sounded an obscenity. Nobody, Chris remembered from her vigil at the window, had 'steamed' more than Bertha herself, when she had occupied a bed in the dormitory.

Fat! Oozing! Pimply! The remembered image flashed through Chris's mind – a dirk unsheathed . . .

'And *you*!' Bertha said, directing her attention to Chris.

'I'm up and dressed,' Chris pointed out, cool, logically, without turning her face from the window.

'ANYHOW!' Bertha withdrew herself on a word which, although bereft of meaning, she could always infuse with threat.

'Little children love ye one another . . .'

Despite long acquaintance with the command on the large text on the wall, signed by St Paul, the girls in the dormitory had never truly 'loved one another'. Self-preservation was their first priority. Urgent, yet fragile and easily shattered.

'First bell's gone,' Chris felt in honour bound to remind her still recumbent colleagues. But without emphasis. Without insistence. Reluctant to let go of the rare moments of privacy that only early morning could bring. Desired always, but essential on Fridays. Band of Hope night.

Hope was indeed the operative word. It had taken the minister time and patience to persuade matron to let the older girls 'out' on Friday evenings on a two-mile walk to the church hall for the weekly temperance meeting.

Matron was no doubt aware that whatever fate the future held for the girls, none of them, at least in this period of their lives, was in any danger of 'drinking themselves to death'. A realist, Matron sensed that there was more danger in a two-mile unchaperoned evening 'outing'.

On top of which, she was a strategist of the first order; with a dash of the subtle, delaying tactics of the first Elizabeth.

Since the minister was also a trustee of the orphanage, his requests were almost impossible to deny. Matron had conceded, 'allowing' the girls to attend the Band of Hope. But with one proviso – depending on the weather!

It was this proviso that kept Chris glued to her position in front of the window, searching for signs in the morning sky. For it didn't need rain itself to cancel the weekly outing. The 'threat' of rain was enough for Matron to defy the minister, and the whole United Free Kirk of Scotland.

Oh! Never had a small girl of fourteen been up against such a powerful adversary. And never was an autumn and winter so full of Fridays which 'threatened rain'! Nor even more the runes of childhood so fervently invoked could diminish the threat:

> Rainie, rainie rattlestanes
> dinna rain on me
> rain on Johnnie Groat's hoose
> far across the sea . . .

Second bell clanging through the dormitory stirred the sleepers into disgruntled wakefulness, and filled the room with complaint. Alice, unaware at last of Chris keeping vigil, and of the reason for such a vigil, shuffled towards the window.

'It's going to rain,' she prophesied. 'It's going to pour! We won't get to the Band of Hope tonight.'

'It could clear up before night,' Chris said, ignoring the gloat that had sounded in Alice's voice. 'It sometimes does,' she reflected, taking a last lingering look at the skyline, before making her way out of the dormitory.

'And,' she reminded Alice, in an attempt to get a little of her own back, 'it's *your* turn to empty all the chamber-pots – except the boys'. I emptied them all yesterday.'

'I always get the dirty jobs,' Alice protested, 'always me!'

'Not always,' Chris pointed out, reaching for the door, anxious to escape the 'my-turn-your-turn' arguments that began each day – '*I* get landed with *most* of the dirty jobs.'

She did too! A fact confirmed when she reached the boys' dormitory for her first task of the morning – stripping their beds, examining the mattresses of the incontinent boys.

No Hamlet was ever forced into reaching a decision such as the one that confronted Chris. To report or not to report that large, damp stain that spread itself across James Dobie's mattress? No thought of nobility troubled her mind. It was the pact that caused her dilemma. Formed between herself and James Dobie in their early years in the orphanage.

'I can't find no bottom to your hunger,' Matron had said of them, anxious, puzzled as if the fault was her own. 'There never seems to be enough for you.'

'Table manners' which they had to memorise in their first weeks in the orphanage had no 'small print' as warning!

> In silence I must take my seat
> and say my Grace before I eat
> Must for my food with patience wait
> Till I am asked to hand my plate
> Must turn my head to cough or sneeze
> And when I ask, say 'if you please'.

I must not speak a useless word
For children should be seen not heard
I must not talk about my food
Nor fret if I don't think it good.
My mouth with food I must not crowd
Nor while I'm eating speak aloud.

When told to rise then I must put
My chair away with noiseless foot
and lift my heart to God above
In praise for all His wondrous love

It never mentioned porridge! Nor the fact that if you didn't eat your porridge you got no tea and bread and butter to follow.

Orphanage porridge, made the night before, so that by morning you could cut it up into thick, lukewarm slices, sent even Chris's voracious, indiscriminate stomach rising up in revolt. James Dobie became her eager and willing receptacle. Thus, the pact was formed. Wolfing down his own portion, while Chris picked warily round the edge of her plate. The transference of plates, with years of practice behind it, was a miracle of dexterity and timing!

All such subterfuges, Chris reflected, never escaped the gimlet eyes of her fellow-orphans, and had to be paid for – help with their home lessons, the coin in demand.

Engulfed in a passing moment of self-pity, assailed by the long-lost, but still remembered freedom of home, Chris struggled towards a decision.

Had James been less incontinent this morning, she would simply have turned his mattress, concealed the 'evidence' and sent up a prayer. 'Don't let Matron be in her examining mood.'

The risk was too great. On Friday, of *all* days, when good behaviour was an unspoken, but important, proviso for attendance at the Band of Hope.

'James Dobie has wet his bed, matron.'

Nobody in the whole wide world could twist a situation with the dexterity of Matron. Chris suddenly found herself the target of Matron's displeasure.

'Did you waken James Dobie last night?'

'Yes, matron'.

'Are you sure?'

'Yes, matron.'

'Did he use his chamber pot?'

'Yes, matron.'

'How do you know he used it?'

'I heard him!'

'Oh traitor untrue,' said the king 'now thou has betrayed me thrice, who would have thought that thou . . .'

James Dobie had not yet learned *Morte D'Arthur* at school, but complete comprehension of it was held within his eyes, accusing Chris from the opposite side of the breakfast table.

The flourish with which he scraped his porridge plate clean, before clasping it firmly to his chest and settling down and back in his chair to concentrate on Chris, dithering around the mess of congealed porridge which now confronted her – no tea, no bread – a dark beginning to an already cloud-threatened day.

'Christina Forbes!'

Bertha's voice broke through the argumentative 'whose-turn-to-do-what' claims that always preceded washing up, and halted Chris in her assertions. For full titles were used amongst themselves only on formal – or foreboding – occasions.

'Matron wants to see you in her sitting-room – at once!'

'It's for something bad?' Her question, tentatively put, was purely rhetorical since it would not be answered by Bertha in her official capacity.

'I *know* it's for something bad.'

Chris flicked swiftly through her memory for recent, but so far undiscovered sins of ommission and/or commission. 'I know. By the sound of your voice.'

'So this,' Matron stood guardian over Chris's opened school-bag on her desk, waving aloft a small, oft-creased bundle of jotter pages, '*this* is why you are always so keen on the Band of Hope. I might have suspected it. Who is this boy who writes that he "can't wait for Friday night"?'

'Till I see you again' – silently Chris completed the sentence for Matron, and, in the doing, recollected every word written on the pages. The lines of 'X's for kisses, the P.S. of regret 'wish they were not on paper, but were real . . .', embarrassment negated by the inner certainty.

'At least there's not *one* dirty thing in the letters . . .'

'A boy at school, Matron – he lives with his grandfather, he's *nearly* an orphan!' Chris volunteered the information in the hope that such a common cause might influence Matron. 'He's got navy stockings with yellow tops . . .' Suddenly she heard herself sharing with Matron the few facts she herself knew about the boy. ' . . . He's got a bike. He can freewheel down Barclay's Brae without once touching his handlebars – you'd like him if you knew him. I know you would!'

Evincing no sign of a shared 'liking', Matron set the pages down on her desk.

'The thing is,' she concluded, after long consideration, 'you're getting too old for the Band of Hope. It's time we were thinking of your *future*. Getting ready for it, when you go into service. There's the old sewing-machine – we could make a start on Friday nights, teaching you to use it – underwear, night-dresses, petticoats, things you'll need when you start your job . . .'

'What punishment?'

Her colleagues clustered around her in the scullery, avid for her downfall.

'None.'

'*No* punishment?' The disbelief in Bertha's voice atoned for much.

'None,' Chris confirmed, thrusting up her sleeves to attack the washing-up. 'I can't be bothered going to the Band of Hope tonight,' she informed them casually. 'I'm getting too old for it, it's for children, Matron says. She's going to teach me to use her *new* sewing-machine.'

'*Her* new sewing-machine?' Bertha asked aghast.

'Her new sewing-machine. To sew my frocks for leaving.'

'Frocks!' Bertha grumbled, 'all *I* had to make was nightgowns and petticoats!'

'You're not *me*,' Chris reminded her, plunging her hands into the sink, '*are* you now?'

> It's raining
> It's pouring
> The old man is snoring.

'Once in Royal . . .'

'It's *Christmas*!'

The jungle drums beat out the information from Hill Street to Lady Lane.

'It's Christmas in Higgins!'

'*Halloween* hasn't even come yet,' Sarah protested. 'Christmas is *ages*.'

'If we don't join *now*,' Ellen, her best friend of the moment, pointed out, 'the Club Cards will be all gone, and we won't get nothing.'

'I haven't got a sixpence to join,' Sarah said.

'Me neither,' Ellen admitted. 'Not till my dad gets his broo money. But we can go up and *look*.'

'Join our Christmas Club NOW!'

The notice in Higgins's window justified Ellen's urgency. The window itself held Sarah entrapped in a confusion of time. As if time had gone back on itself, had whirled towards Christmas before coming to a stop in Higgins's window.

King George and Queen Mary stared as severely from their thrones on the tin tea caddy as they had done in all the remembered Christmases of Sarah's short life.

The toy train in front of the window still looked as if it might whistle off to somewhere, but had not yet decided on its destination.

The doll presiding in the centre of the window had not yet found a mother.

'*Her* shoes are only painted on,' Ellen said. 'Not like *real* shoes. You can't take them off.'

'Not like Mina Scobie's "walkie-talkie" doll,' Sarah agreed. 'It can sleep. Higgins's doll can't. But,' she admitted, 'I've always wanted that doll!'

Unaware as yet, that the doll, the train, the tea caddy were beyond personal possession, reappearing briefly at Christmas time in Higgins's window.

For as the weeks passed, and club members' payments began to falter, until they stopped altogether, an ominous notice appeared in Higgins's window: 'NO REFUND ON LAPSED PAYMENTS'.

'Owing to *clerical* work involved,' Mrs Higgins had once pointed out to Sarah's mother, when she had the temerity to 'object'. '*Clerical* work!' she had snorted to her more timid neighbours, awaiting the outcome of the 'objection', 'some *clerical* work! That old Irish biddy knows how to make two and two into five! That's all she *does* know!'

'*She* wants *doing*!' was always the unaminous verdict of the grown-ups. But their threat was never fulfilled. For, although the figures on Higgins's slate seldom reached an accurate total – 'clerical work' again covering a multitude of Higgins's sins – it had to be endured. Their slate was indispensable.

Nevertheless, Higgins's window always gave timely warning of the spade work that had to be done if Christmas was to be Christmas.

You didn't need sixpence to join the Mission Hall Sunday School nor the junior corps of the Salvation Army. It was timing that counted. Timing, that was important – 'at least a *month* before Christmas,' Ellen insisted. 'For attendance, or we won't be members – and won't get to the Christmas parties!'

'Only cocoa and stale buns,' Sarah said.

'And games!' Sally reminded her, putting in a bit of immediate practice.

'. . . Oh! The grand old Duke of York!
He had ten thousand men
He marched them up to the top of the hill
And he marched them down again.
As they raced together towards the lane.

'And when they were up
They were UP!
And when they were down,
They were DOWN!
And when they were only half way up
They were neither up nor down!'

'The Hill Street bobby's taking down names!' Sarah raced down to the lane to herald the glad tidings. 'I've just seen him. In Kimmer's Wynd. With his red book. The kids are all round him.'

The information needed some consideration: had to be weighed in the balance, since their relationship with the Hill Street bobby was delicate, tenuous when fleetness of foot became their strongest weapon in the small war of attrition that waged between themselves and the bobby – when their song of triumph pursued their pursuer:

'. . . Who would like to be a bobby?
Dressed up in other people's clothes.
Wi' a great big tarry hat
and a belly full o' fat!
And a great big mealie puddin'
for a nose!'

But that was when time was normal. The imminent approach of Christmas, when the Chief Constable's Christmas dinner for poor children was just weeks away, confounded the situation. The bobby's red book, and his threat to take down your name no longer held its menace. Indeed, the thing to be desired was to get your name taken down in the red book, with all possible speed, for the annual Christmas dinner. The fear of your name being omitted – yourself forgotten – cancelled out all other considerations.

'We'd best get ourselves up to Kimmer's Wynd,' Sarah urged the others 'so's the bobby can *see* us!'

'The "H"s to "M"s the night. And I'm "M"!'

'Me too,' Ellen affirmed. 'I'm Menzie. That's an "M".'

'*You're* all right then,' Betsy Kelly assured Ellen. She informed Sarah that 'You're a "Mac" – MacVean – it's the letter that comes after "Mac" that counts. "V" – you'll be about last – there's *hundreds* of "Macs".'

Betsy was right, Sarah realised, as she stood with the other children crowding the court yard behind the police station.

'Blue tickets this year!'

Ellen separated now, on the other side of the yard, by virtue of sure and certain possession of her ticket, held it aloft, waving it across at Sarah.

'*Yellow* tickets last year,' she shouted.

'*Red*!' Cis Tindall contradicted. '*Red* last year.'

'*Yellow*!'

The argument conjoined, rose in tempo until brought to a halt by the ticket bobby –

'NO tickets of any colour till you all SHUT UP!'

MacKenzie . . . MacKellar . . . McKinley . . . McRimmon . . . Macrivey . . . MacRobert . . . MacTavish . . . Her section, thinning out now, increased the panic rising up in Sarah – the feeling of being the last 'M' in the world and apt to be forgotten . . . MacVean . . . Sarah . . .

'*Blue tickets*!' she shouted, squeezing through the crowd in search of Ellen, '*blue tickets*, right enough!'

The ultimate possession of tickets brought a subtle change to the street's inhabitants. Dividing its elders into those who claimed that they 'had *still* some pride left', and ticket-holders whom they accused of 'putting on a poor mouth'.

Friends of a lifetime becoming foes for a fortnight. An attitude which influenced the children.

'We can't play "hoist the green flag"!' Ellen lamented. 'There's not enough for sides. Mina Scobie and Jean Campbell don't play with us any more. Not since we got tickets for the Christmas Dinner!'

'They still play with *me*,' Sarah claimed.

'You're *different*,' Ellen said.

A difference which allowed Sarah a foot in both camps, by virtue of the consensus of opinion of the street's elders: '. . . she's a poor, wee soul. Bless her. No father . . .' A difference which confused Sarah, confronted by an image completely alien to herself. For she had never thought of herself as 'a poor, wee soul'. Nevertheless! The role now thrust upon her was well within her histrionic abilities, albeit hard to act up to when boredom overtook herself and Ellen, and the temptation to disrupt the elders, by playing 'catch as can' along the street, overcame them.

'. . . *You* didn't rap on Annie Frigg's door!' Ellen accused. 'Nor on old Balaclava's door *either*!'

Sarah had begun to realise that obligations could be limiting. She could no longer afford to alienate her champions.

'A *new* frock!' Sarah's mother protested. 'If that's the way of it you'll just have to go without the Christmas Dinner, or else make your way there in your birthday suit!'

The recurring problem of a new frock had raised its anxious head and had once again been resolved, since a new frock simply meant a frock that was new to you! Tentatively donned in the prayerful hope that its original owner would make no further claim on it, accosting you with a shame-making shout – '*my* frock!'

Awkward, wordless. Those brief moments of appraisal of each other. Burnished in finery, lent or given, before lining up in your hundreds behind the kilted pipers for the triumphant march to the town hall through the main streets of the city. Elders and parents, feuds forgotten. Cheering their offspring on as they stepped it out to the music of Scotland the Brave, surging round, then rising up, bearing yourselves within it to some high and proud place of the mind. So that you felt you had really done something fine and brave, though you couldn't quite think what it was. Aware only that getting yourself there at all merited a touch of self esteem!

Racing home together in the early dusk, discarding *all* superfluous things. Fruit, a taste not yet fully acquired, flung to and fro with reckless largesse.

'Want an *orange*?'

'Like an *apple*?'

Holding grimly on to the poke of sweeties. And to the newly minted penny. That talisman, with its shining, never-ending mystery. Proclaiming the date of a year that had not yet arrived.

'It's for *next* year!' Sarah reaffirmed as herself and Ellen stood examining their new pennies in the light of the street lamp. 'Nineteen twenty-four, it says, and it hasn't even come yet!'

'We can't spend it then,' Ellen said. 'Not till next year'.

'I'm not going to spend it!' Sarah vowed, as they raced towards the lane.

'I'm *never* going to spend *mine*!'

'Did you get a fine dinner then?' her mother wanted to know. 'I'm *asking* you! Did you get a fine dinner?'

The dinner itself, although consumed, remained elusive. Untasted in recollection.

'We got an orange,' Sarah said. 'And an apple, a poke of

sweeties, and a new penny. Oh!' she remembered. 'And we all sang "Once in Royal".'

'"David's City",' her mother reminded her. 'It's "Once in Royal *David's City*"!'

The Gowk

You'd felt pity for the Gowk, when yourself was young. And he was a boy – debarred. Clutching the school gates. Engrossed in the rough and tumble of the playground.

In manhood, this on-looking compulsion was still with him. But you had outgrown pity. Revulsion, tinged with apprehension, had taken its place. Until you thought about it, and realised that maybe, maybe the half-witted dribbling boy was now imprisoned grotesquely in the flesh of manhood.

But you didn't often think about that. And certainly the boys on the inside of the school playground never thought about it at all. Ettling always to get out, and within taunting distance of the Gowk.

> We saw Gowkit Jockie
> We saw him run awa
> We saw Gowkit Jockie
> And his nakit Bum and a'!

'Come *inside*, Rob! *And* you, Peter!' Jean Aitken shouted from her kitchen window.

'And stop tormenting the life out of that poor bloody Gowk!' Her father admonished, over her shoulder.

'That "Poor Gowk", as you call him,' Jean Aitken shrugged, 'should have been lockit up and away a long time ago. Terrifying the life out of the bairns.'

'Jockie's harmless enough,' the old man defended. 'He wouldna mind *them*. If they didna keep tormenting *him*!'

'You try telling Kate Riddrie that, Father. She's had her bellyful of the Gowk!'

'That's true enough,' her Father agreed. 'But not until the Gowk's father put the wedding ring on her hand!'

'And she's living to regret *that*!' Jean Aitken pointed out. 'Forbye, the Gowk was but a bairn, then. He's a man. Full-grown, now.'

'. . . and the older he grows, the worse he grows,' Kate Riddrie was complaining. 'He's started to abuse himself again. In broad daylight now! You'd think he hadn't got the wit for *that* even!'

'Maybe it's the instinct he's gotten,' Hugh Riddrie said. 'Even the brute beasts have gotten *that*.'

He had long since found that words failed to justify to himself the existence of his idiot son. And was beginning to discover that they failed even to protect him.

'I could *cope*,' his wife claimed. 'I could *cope* when he was young. But he's getting beyond me now.'

'You could never cope, Kate.' Hugh Riddrie reached above the dresser for his bonnet. 'You could only pretend he wasna there at all.'

'*Better*!' Kate Riddrie flared. 'Than pretending he wasn't an idiot *born*! But then, of course, he's *your* son.'

'So you aye keep reminding me, Kate.'

'And you *need* reminding! Do you know something?'

Hugh Riddrie shook his head. 'No. But I know you're just about to *tell* me something.'

'High time somebody did! You puzzle me,' Kate Riddrie admitted. 'Where other folk would try to keep a Gowk out of sight, *you* seem to like flaunting him in the face of the world.'

'Letting everybody share the *shame*, like, Kate?'

'I don't know what you'd call it!' Kate Riddrie snapped. 'But Nell Crombie was saying that she gets a red face, every time she puts her foot across this door!'

'She would,' Hugh Riddrie agreed. 'A very modest woman, Nell. Forever bragging that her man has never seen her nakit. In his life. Come to think of it,' he reflected, 'neither have you! What the hell is it makes you all so feared to *look*!'

'Decency!' Kate Riddrie said. 'Just plain *decency*!'

'Is *that* the name they've gotten for't? Ah well. I'm aye learning.'

'Not fast enough!' Kate Riddrie shouted, as he made for the door. '*Something's* got to be done. About the Gowk!'

'*Jockie*! *You mean*. Don't you, Kate?' Hugh Riddrie spun round on his heel. '*Jockie*!'

'I meant *Jockie*.' She flustered. 'It was just . . . it was just that everybody else calls him . . .'

'*THE GOWK*!' Hugh Riddrie finished the sentence for her. His quiet anger rising loud. Out of control. 'What do you suggest I do with him, Kate? *Lib* the poor bugger! The way I'd lib a young calf! Or would you have rather I had thrappled him at *birth*! With my bare hands! . . . I've killed a calf for less. For just being shargered . . .'

He could hear the school bairns taunting in the distance. Forcing his forefingers between his teeth, the shrillness of his whistle brought the taunting to a halt. And evoked the memories of the workers on their way home from the farm.

Old Riddrie. Whistling his Gowk again. Poor bugger. Other men had dogs to whistle for. Still. The man himself could be more sociable. Oh, but they minded on Riddrie, young. Another man then. Another man, altogether. That, of course, was before the Gowk was born. They themselves found little enough wrong with the Gowk! A pat on the head. A word in his ear, in the passing. A chew of tobacco slippit into his hand. And God! The Gowk was as happy as if he was in his right mind!

The shrill whistle halted their wives on their way back from the baker's van. Myth and memory blending in a confusion of truth.

The *minute* the Gowk was born. The *instant* the doctor set eyes on him . . . 'Poultice Jimmy', as he was known. For he believed that a bread poultice could cure anything from a blind boil on your bottom to a broken heart. Though a poultice was of little use to the Gowk. But at least the doctor knew *something* was far wrong.

It was the midwife, of course, that had let the cat out of the bag. In *confidence*, mind you! Though she should never have done the like. Not in a job like hers. According to her, the doctor cursed and swore like a tinker when he set eyes on the Gowk. Roaring away at the midwife. To pay heed to the *mother* . . . The midwife swore to the day she died, that Poultice Jimmy *knew*. That he hopit, if they paid no attention to the bairn, it might just dwine away. But the Gowk had survived. Never a day's illness in his life. To the great regret of Mistress Riddrie the Second.

Still. There was nothing on the *women's* consciences. The Gowk, young, had never been debarred from *their* games as girls. Always willing to be 'poor Gracie' lying dead and in her grave. While they circled mournfully around him . . .

> We planted an Apple-tree
> Over his head
> Over his head
> We planted an Apple-tree . . .

. . . 'Did you not hear me the *first* time? I'll comb your hair for you!' Jean Aitken threatened. 'If you don't come inside. And stop crying after that Gowk!'

'The Gowk was following our Liz.' Young Rob dodged his mother's upraised hand. 'Liz didn't see him. That's why Peter and me was shouting. They were going down Sue Tatt's road.'

'Sue Tatt's road!' The information halted Jean Aitken's enraged intention.

'There you are, then!' Dod Aitken laughed. '*There's* something for you to pick your teeth on! We know Sue's not all that particular. But even Sue Tatt would draw the line at the Gowk!'

'Are you *sure*, Rob?' His mother demanded.

'Positive!'

'*Certain*!' Peter added. Enjoying the effect the information had produced. 'We was trying to warn Liz. That's why we was shouting.'

'Our Liz,' Jean Aitken remembered. 'Should have been home by *this* time! The school bus gets in at the back of five. What on earth would Liz be seeking down Sue Tatt's road?'

Liz Aitken, herself, knew what she was seeking. But was not sure whether it was to be found.

'Sue Tatt will know what to do,' Chris Forbes had informed Liz. 'They say she's had more men than we've had suppers.'

That had sounded reassuring enough, last night. But then night had always brought reassurance to Liz. Expecting its very privacy to produce the dark, quiet miracle. And herself waking up. To confirm it, in the morning.

'I've *often* been late,' Chris had said. Sounding it like some special privilege rather than a comfort. 'Sometimes a whole *week* late.'

But then Chris Forbes had never been enticed up into the woods. How glad Liz had always been that she was herself. And not Chris Forbes. Never Chris Forbes. Now, she could have torn Chris right out of her skin. And gone inside it. To be safe. Like Chris was safe.

The rumours surrounding Sue Tatt were such that her house, itself, should have imparted an aura. Secret. Erotic. Its ordinariness disappointed Liz. But then the ordinariness of familiar things had begun to confuse her.

They should *know*. They should look *different*. The thing that had happened to herself should lie distorted, reflected in everything she set eyes on. The skeleton of Rob's bike, stripped of essentials, lying out in the shed. The handles of her father's old plough, curving high above the nettles.

But it was her landscape that was the ultimate traitor. Lochnagar couldn't *stand* there. The Dee it should flood . . .

> The sky it should fall
> Since I am with bairn
> Unwedded and all . . .

'This *friend* . . . this friend of yours, Liz' Sue Tatt asked. 'About how old would she be, then?'

'Sixteen-and-a-half. Nearly seventeen!' Liz extended her age, thinking somehow that it might advance her cause. 'Chris Forbes said you could help!'

'Oh she *did*, did she? It could be nothing, Liz,' Sue Tatt concluded, transforming her irritation with Chris Forbes into an attempt to reassure Liz Aitken. 'That whiles happens to young lassies. Till they become regular, like.'

'But I *am* regular!' Liz protested. 'I've always been regular. Till *now*.'

'Oh Liz! Liz Aitken. Not *You*!'

The roof at home would have fallen in, under such an admission. It was the ec'o of its fall that sounded in Sue Tatt's voice.

'But you could *help*!' Liz urged. 'Everybody says . . .'

'Everything except their prayers, Liz. The thing is,' Sue stood pondering the paradox. 'Everybody knows the cure. Till the ailment happens. Syne, they know nothing. For *myself*,' Sue recollected, 'I just fell back on the old Penny Royal. Quinine. And the skin of my legs peeling off in a pail of hot water and mustard. Knowing they were all useless. But always just . . . hoping. Nothing ever budged mine an inch! Not until they were good and ready to be born. But cheer *up*, Liz! It *could* be a "wrong spy"! And I've had my share of them! You might just waken up the morn's morning to find that everything's just fine, again. And oh, whatten a fine feeling *that* is, Liz, stroking yourself under the sheet. As if your hands loved your body again. And the sweat pouring out of you. With relief, just. And thanking God. Even though you're not a Christian. Because you cannot think of anybody else to thank. And promising never to do it again. Not as long as you live . . . But of course you'll do it again, Liz!' Sue Tatt bent towards her, laughing. Pressing her hands on Liz's shoulders, as if they might leap up, and dance together, to a bright reel of Sue's composing. 'Again. And again, Liz! And it will be *right* then. And fine. For some lad will have *wedded* you! There's no chance of *this* lad wedding you?' Sue asked, as if the music itself had ended, and the bright bubble of hope drifted high up. Out of mind's reach.

'*None!*' That was a certainty. And Liz merely confirmed it. 'He's sitting his Highers,' she explained, 'and I'm trying for a Bursary. I'm going to the University. My mother's *set* on that. And my father will kill me. You'll not tell!' she urged. For, although hope had gone, secrecy still seemed essential. 'You'll never tell.'

'I'll not tell', Sue Tatt promised. 'But you should, Liz. Tell your mother. And tell quick! Before other folk get in there first. That's what "gets" mothers. Not having the time to get their faces ready. To look on the world again.'

'It's my *father*!' Liz rose to go. 'He'll kill me. When he finds out.'

'I doubt that, Liz. I very much doubt that!'

'You don't know my father.'

Liz Aitken could well be right, Sue Tatt thought, as she watched Liz turn the bend of the road. But still Sue doubted. It was with the *mothers* of the parish that she had a mere 'nodding acquaintance'.

'A fine night, again, Jockie!' Sue Tatt cried out to the Gowk, as he shambled past her gate. Poor silly creature, he wouldn't understand a word she was saying. But he might just know that somebody was speaking to him. 'Another fine night again, Jockie!'

The brambles down in the King's Howe were always the first to ripen. Liz Aitken stood amongst the bushes, caught up once more in a deceptive sense of security. The taste of childhood on her tongue. The colour of it staining her mouth. Savouring a fallacy.

The reeshling in the bushes behind her didn't disturb her peace of mind. It was the unseen hands that gripped her shoulders, that sent her cry rising across the Howe.

Such cries breaking the silence of the quiet Howe were common enough. Easily enough analysed by listeners in the passing. A screaming rabbit cornered at last by the watchful weasel. A bleating ewe worried by a stray dog. The black sweep of the Hoodie Crow. And the rising protest of its victim. Distress traced easily enough to its unseen source. It was the source, itself, that could always momentarily stop the listening heart.

The Gowk, was no solitary. Hugh Riddrie nearly always knew where to find him. The smiddy, the general shop, the bus stop. For Jockie liked to be amongst folk. A pity, that. For folk either ignored his presence. Or acknowledged it, the way they acknowledged old Moss, the shepherd's dog. With a pat on the head.

In all the years, Hugh Riddrie had never got rid of the ache that caught at him at the sight of his son, standing with, but not of, normal men. It was rare. But easier, at times like now, when they came upon each other alone. In the nakedness of their relationship. When communication, though primitive, was natural. When tone of voice transcended interpretation. And monologue, comprehended by the listener, gave release to the speaker.

'*There* you are, Mannie! I've been whistling on you all night.
What have you been up to, Jockie?
Riving head first amongst the bushes!
Steady! Steady now! Till I get you wipit down.
Let's see your mouth now! You've been dribbling again!
The moustache of you's all slavers!
Steady now! Steady *on*!
Your flies are wide open again! Will you *never* learn to button
    yourself up!

You know fine that drives her clean mad.
She's gotten such a spite to flies.
Especially open flies.
STILL!
You're *fine*, now!
In you go, then, Jockie.
Up the stairs. As nippit as you can!
Hold it! Hold it, Jockie. Till I get the boots off you.
That's *it*! *That's* it!
She'll not hear you, now.
We'll better her, this time!
Eh, Jockie? Eh, Mannie!
In you go, then! You're fine, now.
All present and correct!
NO! Jockie, *NO*!
Let my hand *go*.
I'm *coming* in! Right *behind* you.
Let my hand *go*!
Do you not *see*, Jockie?
You've got to go in *first*!
As if you'd been a *good* mannie!
And come all the way home. By *yourself*!
It's easier, that way, Jockie.
In you go then. We'll be all right!'

'It's all *wrong*! All wrong, I tell you!' Jean Aitken insisted. 'That Gowk should never be allowed to roam the countryside. Just look at the state Liz has come home in. Are you all *right*, Liz? What did that mad bugger of a Gowk *do* to you?'

'We tried to warn Liz,' Young Rob remembered. '*And* me!' Peter confirmed. 'We was shouting after the Gowk.'

'Off up to your beds! The pair of you!' Jean Aitken commanded. 'Are you *sure* you're all right, Liz? Are you *sure*!'

'Liz will be all right.' Rob Aitken said. 'She got a fleg just.'

'She's gotten more than a fleg! She's looking *terrible*.'

'He grabbed me,' Liz explained. 'And I didn't see him. *That*'s what it was. I didn't *see* him. I ran all the way from the King's Howe. But I thought I'd never get out of the spot.'

'What took you down to the King's Howe, like?' her father asked. 'That's bit out of your road, isn't it?'

'My homework. I forgot to take it down. I went over to get it from Chris Forbes.'

'I wouldn't bother about homework the night,' Jean Aitken advised. 'You should hold straight on up to your bed. You've had a gey shake-up.'

'I'll be all right. I couldn't sleep if I went to my bed.'

'Liz is right!' her Father agreed. 'Stop fussing her, woman!'

'Well then!' Jean Aitken turned in attack on both of them. 'If she's all right, and can't go up to her bed, and can't sleep, she's *not* going to sit molloching here all night! She can just take herself through to the sink. And make a start to the washing-up!'

She would 'tell them on Saturday'. The decision taken, Liz leant against the sink, comforted by the postponement of time that lately she had begun to allow herself, when days could seem almost normal.

'I could have sworn I put preserving ginger down on the grocer's list.' Her mother's voice drifted through to the scullery. 'I'm sure I noticed some at the back of the press, the other day . . .'

There *couldn't* be anything wrong with Liz! Her mother would *know*. She would never be worrying about preserving ginger, if there *was* something wrong . . .

'But I think it's *last* year's preserving ginger that's in the press. The strength will have gone out of it . . .'

If there *was* something wrong, her mother would stop going on about preserving ginger forever . . .

'I could be speaking to *myself*!' her mother was complaining to

her father. 'I *told* you she would be better off in her bed! Standing
through there in a dwam. She's had a bigger upset than she'll
admit. And if it's the last thing I do, I'll make Hugh Riddrie's ears
blister! Him and that Gowk of his.'

The Gowk, himself, was beginning to take on a subtle new
dimension in the eyes of the Howe. A curious kind of normality.
An ability to share in the venial sins of ordinary men. It was Liz
Aitken who began to lose dimension to its inhabitants.

You could have 'knocked them all down with a feather', they
swore. Liz Aitken of *all* people. And her set to sit for the bursary.
She was just about the *last*! Not that anybody was perfect, of
course. But Liz Aitken was . . .

'As liable as the *next* one!' Teen Rait had snapped, in an
attempt to keep her own image of perfection intact. God help
whoever was the father, they agreed. It was bound to be somebody. *That* was for certain. Though it had happened *once*. Just
once. But that was two thousand years ago. And, though they
were regular kirk-goers, and believed in every word the psalms
uttered, they'd just never quite managed to 'swallow *that* one'. It
was for papes. Although Cis Coutts, the simple creature, had tried
it on when *she* was pregnant. And syne forgot. And admitted to
the doctor that she 'had pink knickers on at the time'. Still, and
seriously, though, God help whoever was the father when Rob
Aitken got his hands on him. He couldn't get a word out of Liz
herself. She wouldn't say a cheep. There was a rumour. Only a
rumour, mind you! But then, there always was. They would have
died without one. A 'speak'. Oh! A *whisper* just. That it was – *the
Gowk*.

'You haven't got Liz to admit it, yet, then?' Kate Riddrie asked.
    'No.' Jean Aitken shook her head. 'But she will. The state Liz
came home in, that night. Her jumper torn, her legs scratit. And
herself, nearly hysterical . . .'

'I can believe *that*! Your Liz would never have had the strength against a brute-beast like the Gowk!'

'Never a one for the lads, Liz. Her head aye buried in some book, just . . .'

'I was saying Liz would never have had the strength! Something will have to be done about the Gowk, *now*! And you've gotten witnesses!'

'Aye some book, just . . .'

'You've gotten witnesses!' Kate Riddrie urged.

'Young Rob. And Peter. They were trying to warn Liz.'

'WELL! THEN! That's *it*!'

'She never crossed the door at night. Except whiles. Down to Chris Forbes for her homework.'

'You've gotten *witnesses*! All it needs now, is to testify before the board!'

'But Liz. Liz is so unwilling. So unwilling to do that! Do you think? Do you think, maybe . . .?' Jean Aitken hesitated, unable to put her own apprehension into words. 'Maybe, it's because he is a *Gowk*?'

'That's where you've *got* him!' Kate Riddrie got to her feet, in triumph. 'That's what I'm trying to *tell* you. It's Liz's word against a Gowk's word. And he's got none. At least none that anybody could make any sense out of. Forbye! The whole Howe can testify that the Gowk's forever shambling all over the place. *Exposing* himself!'

'You'll be satisfied *now* then Kate. You've gotten your will. You've gotten rid of Jockie, at last . . .'

'*My* first job. The first fine day. Will be to get that stinking mattress of his outside. And set fire to it.'

'*That* was what you always wanted, Kate . . .'

'It stank the house to high heaven.'

'Wasn't it, Kate?'

'At least we'll get a bit of fresh air into the house, at last . . .'

'Speak! You *bitch*! Or have you lost your tongue! A damned pity you didn't lose it in front of the board!'

'It wasn't *me* that got rid of the . . . *Jockie*'.

'NO! But you said damn all to prevent it!'

'What could *I* say to prevent it? The board could see for themselves. Liz Aitken's belly was getting big enough!'

'*Jockie* didn't make it so.'

'You've got no *proof* of that.'

'Nor of the *t'other*!' Hugh Riddrie concluded, making for the door. 'All that Jockie ever wanted was for somebody to *speak* to him.'

'*Speak* to him!' Kate Riddrie snorted. 'What on earth can anybody say to a GOWK!'

'I'll tell you what they can say to a Gowk, Kate! I'll *tell* you.'

Hugh Riddrie turned to face her. Searching dumbly for words, that could be put into words. *Knowing* them. Thousands of them. Words that often weren't words at all, but instincts. Transmitted by tone and touch. A language acquired and mastered in a confusion of pain and frustration.

'You can say *anything* to a Gowk, Kate!' The realisation took him by surprise. 'Anything at all. That's the best thing about Gowks. They never tell. And that's the worst thing about them. They cannot tell. But I'll find somebody, Kate. I'll find somebody who *can* tell!'

. . . Liz Aitken O Liz Aitken . . .

'Come on, Liz! Come on, lass,' her mother persuaded. 'Moping around the house like this is doing you no good. No good at all. And it such a fine night. Why don't you take yourself off for a bit walk?'

'Because she's feart!' Young Rob blurted out. Unable to contain his knowledge.

'*FEART?*'

'That's right!' Peter confirmed. '*Feart*!'

... Liz Aitken O Liz Aitken ...

'Feart of what, Liz!' It was her own fear that Jean Aitken probed. Convinced that such a fear had not touched her daughter. Oh, but the young were lucky. One danger at a time. Clear and cut. Over and done with. With little hindsight – and not very much foresight. If only the father had been a normal lad. And not a Gowk. 'Feart of *what*, Liz?'

'Nothing. Nothing, just.'

... Liz Aitken O Liz Aitken ...

'Well then!' Jean Aitken urged. 'Off into the fresh air with you. Young Rob and Peter will go with you for company.'

'Never *ME*!'

'ME *neither*!' Peter echoed his brother's determination. 'The other bairns will cry after us! "Gowk's bairn! Gowk's bairn!" *That's* what they'll cry.'

'Is that right, Liz?' her Father asked. 'Is that what they cry?'

'Sometimes. It's only the bairns, though.'

... Liz Aitken O Liz Aitken ...

'I wouldn't let that worry you, Liz. Folk have always needed somebody to cry after. And they've got no Gowk, now.'

'If only it had been some other lad ...' Regret slipped out of Jean Aitken's control. And sounded itself in her voice.

'Some *other* lad!'

Her father's astonishment confirmed Liz's own certainty.

'If it had been some *other* lad, Liz would have been out of here. *Bag* and *baggage*! What happened was no fault of her own. It took half a dozen of us grown men, to hold the Gowk down, till they got him off to the asylum.'

'Come on, Liz. Up you get.' Her mother piloted her towards the door. 'Just you take a turn round the steading. I used to like fine a walk when darkness was coming down,' her mother confided, as they stood on the doorstep. 'I suppose I felt ashamed in daylight. *Not* because I was carrying a bairn, Liz. But just I felt so ungainly. And ugly in myself. Still!' her arm found her daughter's shoulder. 'Every creature's *bonnie* when it's little, Liz.'

A daft thing to say, Jean Aitken thought, as she watched Liz from the door. The wrong words sometimes came out. When you couldn't find the right ones to say.

'Just the length of the steading, Liz!' she called out, reminding her daughter . . .

But the Gowk's father roamed freely enough. On the prowl. Night after night. They said. Neither Gowk to whistle on, nor dog for company. His croft running to wreck and ruin. His oats rotting in the stack. And the threshing mill had gone long since past his road end. His turnips neither howked nor stored for his cattle-beasts. And winter nearly on top of the man. Bad enough when his first wife died, and the Gowk was born. Worse than ever *now* since they'd carted the Gowk off to the asylum.

Come to think of it, they themselves missed the Gowk. You would never believe *that*! But they'd just got used to him, like. Popping up here and there. And everywhere around the Howe. Still. It was an ill wind. And it had fair suited *Katie Riddrie*!

'I'm not so sure that it did!' Meg Tait informed them. 'I'm not so sure at all! Kate Riddrie *herself* was telling me only the other day . . .'

'There's no living with him. No living with him at all. On the prowl all night. And sitting amongst my feet all day. Never taking his eyes off me. And never opening his mouth to me. Just mumbling away yonder to himself. He aye maintained that his first wife was at fault for the bairn being born a Gowk. But I'm beginning to have my doubts. The way he sits mumbling to himself. He'd aye gotten such an *obsession* with that Gowk.'

. . . Liz Aitken O Liz Aitken . . .

LIZ!

So it hadn't been merely in her imagination. Or, maybe it had been created out of her imagination.

LIZ AITKEN!

Strange how prepared she was . . . 'I'm in a hurry, Mr Riddrie.'
'Aye, Liz. You've been in a great hurry this past few weeks!
What is it that you're running from like?
Hold on, Liz! Just hold *on*, there!
You're not *feart* are you, Liz?
No! Of course you're not feart!
You know fine that the *Gowk* canna jump out on you the night.
No. He canna do that. He's far enough away, the night.
You made sure of that!
You *all* made sure of it. The whole bloody jing bang of you!
No! No! Liz! Hold on!
It wasn't Jockie? Was it, now?'

'I told the board . . .'

'I know damned fine what you told the *board*!
You try telling *ME*!
Struck suddenly dumb are you, Liz?
It's some late in the day for that.
It was never Jockie, Liz. *Never* Jockie.
You see Liz, he wouldn't even have kent *where* to *PUT* the bloody thing.
But *I* ken, Liz.

I ken *for* him.'

The Bridge

For the first time in his eight years, he had caught the biggest tiddler. A beezer it was. Even Mike – the tiddler champ – grudgingly admitted its superiority.

'But maybe it's the jam jar that makes it look so big,' Mike qualified.

'Some kinds of glass makes things look bigger.'

It *wasn't* the glass that made it look bigger. He had urged Mike to look inside the jam jar. And there swam surely – the king of tiddlers.

'*I* don't reckon it much.'

Anxious to keep on Mike's side, Tich McCabe peered into the jar. 'And Mungrel doesn't reckon it much either. Do you, Mung?'

Mungrel, who never spoke until somebody else put words into his mouth, agreed with Tich, 'S'right. I don't reckon it much neither.'

'Could easy not be a tiddler at *all*!'

Dave Lomax shouted from his perch on the branch of the tree. 'Could just be a trout. A wee trout!'

' – Could be . . .' Mung echoed; for although he had never set eyes on a trout he was in agreement with the others to 'disqualify' the tiddler.

'Let's *go* men!' Mike commanded. Suddenly tiring of the discussion.

'Scarper! First to reach the chain bridge. Is the *greatest*!'

'You're not some kind of wee trout.' He protested. Running to catch up with them.

'You're *not*. . . .'

He stopped running to peer into his jam jar to reassure its occupant.

'You're a *tiddler*. And you're the *biggest* tiddler we've catched the day.'

'*Hold* it, men!' he shouted to the others. 'Wait for me.'

The authority in his voice surprised himself. Usually he was content enough to lag behind the others. Tolerated by them, because he was handy for doing all the things they didn't like to do themselves. Like swiping his big brother's fag ends. And ringing the bell of the school caretaker's door. Or handing over his pocket money to 'make up the odds' for a bottle of 'juice'. But *today* he was one of them. He had caught the biggest tiddler.

It was when he caught up with them at the bridge that his newly found feeling of triumph began to desert him.

'O.K. tiddler champ,' Mike said.

'Gi' us the jar. We'll guard the tiddler.'

'Yeah. Give,' Mung echoed.

'It's *your* turn to span the bridge,' Dave said.

He grasped his jar firmly against his anorak. He didn't need anybody to guard his tiddler. He didn't want to span the bridge either! *Nobody* spanned the bridge until they were *ten* at least! The others had never before expected *him* to span the bridge. He had always raced across it – the safe way – keeping guard over all the tiddlers while the others spanned it.

'*Your* turn,' Mike was insisting. '*We* have spanned it. Hundreds of times.'

'*Thousands* of times!' Dave amended.

'Even *Mungrel* spans it,' Tich reminded him. 'Don't you Mung? And Mungrel's even tichier than me!'

'Mungrel's *eleven*,' he pointed out. 'I'm not even nine yet.'

'Only . . . Mungrel's not *chicken*!' Mike said. 'Are you, Mung? You're not chicken.'

'I'm not chicken *neither*!' he protested. 'I'm *not* chicken.'

'O.K. O.K.!' they said. Beginning to close in on him. '*O.K.*! So you're not chicken! . . . *Prove* it . . . just prove it . . . that's *all*! Span the bridge and *prove* it.'

He knew how to span the bridge all right. Sometimes – sometimes kidding on that he was only 'mucking around' he practised a little. Spanning the part of the bridge that stood above the footpath. Knowing that even if he fell he would still be safe – safe as he felt *now*. Knowing that the ground was under his dangling legs.

Left hand over right – left over right – all his fear seemed to have gone into his hands. All his mind's urgings could scarcely get them to keep their grip of the girder.

Left over right – left over –

The river's bank was beneath him now. Dark pools flowed under the bank, he remembered. Pools where the tiddlers often hid – the *biggest* tiddlers. Sometimes he had caught them just sitting bent forward on the bank. Holding his jam jar between his legs. His bare feet scarcely touching the water. He'd felt afraid then, too. A *different* kind of fear. Not for himself. Just of things which his eyes couldn't see. But which his hands could feel. Things that brushed against them . . . Grasping and slimy.

He would never have been surprised, if, when he brought up his jam jar to examine its contents, he discovered neither tiddler nor tadpole inside it, but some strange creature, for which nobody had yet found a name.

Left over – right – left –

The shallows were beneath him now. Looking, even from this height, as safe as they had always looked. His *feet* had always told him how safe the shallows were. A safety – perfect in itself – because it was intensified by surrounding danger.

You could stand, he remembered, with one foot in the shallows, your toes curling round the small stones. While your other foot sank into the sand – down and down . . .

Left over right, left over right – over –

He had a feeling that his body would fall away from his arms and hands long before he reached the end of the bridge.

Left over right – over.

It might be easier that way. Easier just to drop down into the water. And leave his hands and arms clinging to the bridge. All by themselves.

Left over – right.

He was at the middle of the river now. That part of it which they said had no bottom. That could be *true*, he realised. Remembering how, when they skimmed their stones across the water, into the middle, the stones would disappear. But you could never hear them *sound* against the depths into which they fell.

Mike had once said that, though the water *looked* as quiet as anything – far down, where you couldn't see, it just kept whirling round and round, waiting to suck anybody at all down inside it . . .

– over – right – left –

He wouldn't look down again. He wouldn't look down *once*. He would count up to fifty. The way he always counted to himself – when bad things were about to happen.

One two three four five six . . . Better to count in tens, he wouldn't lose his 'place' so easily that way –

One . . . two . . . three . . . four . . . five . . . six seven eight.

He thought he could hear the voice of the others. He must be past the middle of the bridge, now – the water beneath him was still black but he could see shapes within it.

The voices were coming nearer. He knew that they were *real*.

'CHARGE! MEN!' Mike was shouting. '*CHARGE!*'

He could hear them reeshling up the rivers bank. And their feet clanking along the footpath. They were running away . . . Ever since he could remember the days had ended with them all running away. Only *this* time, his tiddler would be with them too. And Mike would boast that *he* had catched it. He had almost forgotten about the tiddler. And it no longer seemed to matter.

Green and safe, the bank lay below him. He could jump down now. But he wouldn't. Not yet! It was only tiches like Mungrel, that leapt down from the girder, the moment they saw the bank beneath them.

Mike never did that. He could see, clear as anything in his mind's eye, how Mike always finished spanning the bridge, one hand clinging to the girder, the other gesturing, high, for a clear runway for himself before swooping down to earth again with cries of triumph!

'*Bat* Man! *Bat* Man!'

Until Such Times

'They're coming the day.' Grandmother bustled into the kitchen, waving a letter aloft. 'Postie's just brought a line. Now! If,' she said, pausing to consider the matter, '*If* they were to catch the through train, they should manage to win here in time for a bite of dinner.'

'I'd be the better of a clean shawl, then,' the Invalid Aunt suggested, 'if they're coming the day.'

– A suggestion that stripped Grandmother clean of the good humour that had been over her. 'My hands are never out of the wash tub!' she snapped. 'The shawl that's on you is clean enough! It's barely been on your back a week! And, as for *you*! . . .' Grandmother's face bent down till it was level with your own. '*You* can just sup up your porridge! There's a lot of work to be got through. If they're coming the day. Your Aunt Millie and Cousin Alice.'

'A lot of help she'll be to you. That one!' the Invalid Aunt said. 'Her Cousin Alice is a different kettle of fish. Another bairn altogether. Well brought up. And biddable.'

'Alice is neither better nor worse than any other bairn!' Grandmother snorted, before turning in attack on you again. 'And there's no call for you to start banging the teapot on the table!'

'The din that one makes,' the Invalid Aunt grumbled, 'is enough to bring on one of my heads!'

'For pity's sake, Edith! She's only a bairn.'

Times like these, you loved Grandmother. Knowing she was on your side. Times like these, you hated the Invalid Aunt. Sat huddled in her shawl on the bed-chair by the window. The smell

of disinfectant always around her. And that other smell of commode. The medicine bottles along the window-sill for when 'the
head came on her' or 'the heart took her'. Even the Invalid Aunt's
medicine bottles had taken on malevolence, getting you off to a
bad start with Grandmother, at the very beginning of your stay.

'You *understand*! You understand, bairn. I'm telling you
NOW! And I don't want to have to tell you again! You must
never touch your Aunt Edith's medicine bottles. Never!
Ever!'

'But she said the heart took her!'

'Not even when the heart takes her,' Grandmother had insisted.
'Mind you on that! you must never touch Aunt Edith's medicine
bottles. Not as long as you are here!'

But you weren't here to stay forever! Your Aunt Ailsa had
promised you that. You was only here to stay . . . 'Until Such
Times', Aunt Ailsa had said on the day she took you to Grandmother's house . . . 'Until Such Times as I can find a proper place
for you and me to bide. For you should be at school. But the
authorities would just go clean mad if they found out they had a
scholar who lived in a Corporation lodging house. And spent
most of her time in the Corporation stables. Sat between the two
dust cart horses! SO You are going to school. And biding with
Grandmother . . . Until Such Times . . .' You could never tell
when Until Such Times had passed. But you began to recognise its
passing. With Grandmother bringing each week to an end, always
on the scold, on Sunday mornings.

'Learning your catechism on the *Sabbath*! Five minutes before
you set off for the Sunday School! I told you to learn it last
night!'

But you had learned it 'last night'. You knew it 'last night'. 'It's
just . . .' you tried to explain to Grandmother, 'it's just the words.
They might all change in the night. I'm looking up to make
sure!'

'It's just . . .' Grandmother always maintained, 'it's just that you didn't put your mind to it, last night! So! Let's hear it now, then! What is the Chief End of Man?'

'Man's Chief End is to glorify God and enjoy Him forever – '

It was the coming of the dark night that told you summer was at an end. 'A *candle*!!! A candle up to her *bed*!' The Invalid Aunt had protested, prophesying that 'They would all be burned alive in their sleep!' And so paving the way for Grandmother's instant rejection of your request for a candle. 'It was only,' Grandmother had pointed out, 'the shadows of the fir trees that you've seen, moving against your window, and you should be used to that by this time! There was nothing,' she tried to assure, 'nothing to be feared of in the wood. It's a blithe place for a bairn. Wait you!' she had exhorted. 'Just wait you till summer comes round again!' – an exhortation that had dismayed you, that had extended time beyond all comprehension of its passing self.

'I'm *saying*!' Grandmother grabbed the teapot from your hands. 'I'm saying there's a lot of work to be got through. With your Aunt Millie and Cousin Alice already on their road!'

'If it had been *Ailsa* that was coming,' the Invalid Aunt said, she would have jumped to it! My word! She would that!'

But it *wasn't* your Aunt Ailsa that was coming. She never 'dropped a line'. She just arrived. Unexpected. Unannounced.

How you wished that she could have arrived unseen. That the wood, which hid everything else, could have hidden Aunt Ailsa, too. But the kitchen window looked out on the road, and on all who passed along it, and the Invalid Aunt's voice was always the first to rise up in forewarning. 'God help us! *She*'s on her way! Ailsa! Her ladyship! Taking up the whole of the road. Looks like she went into the Broadstraik Inn. And didn't come out till closing time!'

How you wanted to leap up off your stool, and hurtle yourself down the road to warn Aunt Ailsa. 'Walk straight, my Aunt Ailsa. Walk as straight as you can! They've seen you coming. They're all watching behind the curtains.'

'Thank God it's not Ailsa that's coming,' the Invalid Aunt concluded. 'We can do fine without her company!'

For once, you found yourself in agreement with the Invalid Aunt. Albeit with a sense of betrayal, and a pain for which you had not found the source, hidden somewhere, within the memory of your Aunt Ailsa's last – and first – 'official' visit.

You had recognised the man and his pony and trap, waiting at the small wayside railway station, but had not realised that he, too, was awaiting the arrival of your Aunt Ailsa. Not until he came towards you, in greeting . . . 'You mind on me? Surely you mind on me!' he had insisted, flummoxed by your silence. 'You'll mind on the pony then! I'll warrant you've forgotten the pony's name.'

'He's Donaldie,' you said, willing enough to claim acquaintance with the pony. 'He's Donaldie. His name's Donaldie.'

The cat, Aunt Ailsa grumbled, as the man elbowed her towards the trap, must have got her tongue, for this was a poor welcome, considering Aunt Ailsa had come all this way.

It was the man! you protested. HIM. Donaldie's dad. 'He belongs to his pony! Not to US. Not to you and me!'

It was only when they reached the wood that the old intimacy warmed up between them. Whoaing Donaldie to a halt, Aunt Ailsa spoke in the tone of time remembered, when the world was small enough to hold what she used to describe as . . . you and me. Ourselves two. And the both of us . . .

'You know,' Aunt Ailsa had confided, 'how Grandmother hates me smoking my pipe. So we're just going to take a turn up the wood for a smoke. I want you to do a small thing for me. To bide here, and keep an eye on Donaldie. We'll not be long. About five minutes just,' she emphasised, presenting you with another aspect of time.

'Five minutes *must* be up now, Donaldie,' you confided to the pony, munching away on the grass verge. His calm acceptance of passing time beginning to distress you, since animals differed from yourself in appearance only, never in understanding. 'It must be up, Donaldie. I've counted up to hundreds.'

'I know something about you, Donaldie,' you boasted, beginning to be irritated by the pony's indifference. 'Something about all horses. Something my Aunt Ailsa once told me. All horsemen have a secret word of command. 'The horseman's *knacking* word,' she called it. But no horseman will ever tell the secret word. He would lose his power, that way of it. I don't know the secret word,' she admitted to the pony. But you might know it, Donaldie. If I could just find it.'

Time poised upon, and passing within, all the words you could remember. Tried out and tested, with no reaction from the pony.

'Maybe,' you suggested at last, 'maybe the secret word's in Gaelic . . . Ay Roh. Ay Roh

'El Alooran
El Alooran

Ay Roh Ay Roh
Ay Roh'

'Stop wheebering away to yourself, there!' Aunt Ailsa commanded, as they turned up the track to Grandmother's house. 'And pay attention to what I am telling you! Not a word out of your head to Grandmother. Not one word about Donaldie's dad! We never saw him the day. We never set *eyes* on him. Just you mind on that.'

'Mind now,' Grandmother was saying, 'When your Cousin Alice comes the day, just you play quiet in the clearing. You know how her mother hates Alice getting her clothes all sossed up in the wood.'

'That one wouldn't worry,' the Invalid Aunt assured Grandmother. 'She would rive in the bushes till she hadn't a stitch to her back. It's high time she took herself through to the scullery and made a start on the dishes!'

'You cannot expect her to be stood out in the cold scullery all morning!' Grandmother snapped.

'But I'm needing the commode!' the Invalid Aunt protested. 'I'm needing to pay a big visit. And I can't do a thing! Not with that one. Stood there. All eyes!'

'She's taking no notice, Edith! She's got better things to look at, than you sat stuck there on the commode. Come on, bairn!' Grandmother said, elbowing you out of the kitchen. It's time you and me took a turn up the wood for a burthen of kindlers. And a breath of fresh air!'

'I'm needing the commode.' The Invalid Aunt's whine followed them to the porch door. 'I'm leaking! You know fine I can't contain!'

I can contain
I've never wet myself
Nor ever will again

'*That*!' Grandmother said, when she caught up with you at the clearing, 'is a bad thing to say. And a worse thing to *think*!'

'I beg pardon.' Your apology was instant. And genuine. Moments shared alone with Grandmother were too rare, too precious, to be wasted in acrimony.

'I grant you grace,' Grandmother acknowledged, spreading herself down and across the log. 'But, if that's what they're learning you at the school . . .'

School, like Grandmother herself, was a separate thing, and shared only at times like these, beyond influence of the house and the Invalid Aunt.

'If,' you said, squeezing yourself down on the log beside her, 'if we were sitting out in the porch, on a fine summer evening, and a weary, thirsty traveller came by and begged us for a drink of milk. And he had wings instead of ears. And wings instead of feet. Do you know what that man's name would be?'

'Wings instead of ears, did you say!'

'And wings instead of feet!' you reminded Grandmother.

'No,' she admitted. 'You've gotten me fair beat there! I've never heard tell of that man before!'

'His name would be Mercury. He's in my school reader. He can fly all round the world in a minute!'

'I can well believe that!' she conceded. 'With all that wings he's gotten.'

In moments like that, with the mood of acceptance over Grandmother, a positive admission of time, and its passing, seemed feasible.

'I wouldn't need a candle at night, now,' you boasted. 'I'm not feared of the wood, now.'

'Of course you're not feared,' Grandmother agreed. 'The nights are stretching out, now.'

'I still wouldn't need a candle!' you insisted. 'But that's *one* thing! I won't be here when the dark nights come again. That's *one* thing!' you claimed, jumping down off the log. 'I won't be here when the dark nights come again. Do *you* think I'll still be here when the dark nights come again?'

'That's hard to say,' Grandmother pulled herself up off the log, and stood, considering. 'Hard to tell. But *no*! she decided at last. 'No. I should hardly think you'd still be here, when the dark nights come again.'

> Until Such Times
> As we go home
> A Hundred Hundred miles
> And all the People
> They bow down
> And everybody smiles . . .

'I know,' Cousin Alice claimed, when they reached the clearing, 'I know why Grandfather says we mustn't go down through the woods where the men are working.'

'So do I though,' you assured her. 'It's because they *swear*! Something cruel! Grandmother says it's because they come from the south. And I know the swear the men say! It's a terrible swear. It begins with F! But mind!' you urged Cousin Alice. 'Don't you say it. *Ever*! They would just murder *me*! For telling!'

She hadn't heard that word before, Cousin Alice admitted. But you had heard it. Hundreds of times. In the Corporation lodging house. It didn't sound terrible then. Just like all the other words. It didn't sound terrible, until one day in the wood, when one of the wood men shouted it out.

'You should have seen the look on Grandfather's face!' you said to Cousin Alice. 'I wanted to cry out to him . . . it wasn't me that swore, Grandfather! It wasn't *me*! Just to make Grandfather speak to me. For once. And to let him know that I don't swear. And I wanted to stand as quiet as anything, so that the twigs wouldn't crackle, and Grandfather wouldn't see me at all. Sometimes,' you confessed to Cousin Alice, 'sometimes I'm never sure what to do . . .'

'Ankle strap shoes, like what Alice has got! Whatever would you be wanting next!' the Invalid Aunt wondered. 'Alice's Mother and Father worked hard for Alice's shoes!' she informed you. 'And Alice took good care of them when she got them!'

'Sorrow be on shoes!' Grandmother snapped. 'The lark needs no shoes to climb to heaven. Forbye!' she assured you. 'Thin shoes like yon wouldn't last you a week in this wood!'

'They wouldn't last you a day!' the Invalid Aunt said. 'But then, there's just no comparison!'

She would like you to be jealous of Alice, the Invalid Aunt. And that was the strange thing, although you envied Alice's shoes, you was never jealous of Alice herself. But glad for her. Proud of her. Willing to claim acquaintanceship. The glory that was Alice,

somehow reflecting on yourself . . . Look everybody! Just look!
This is Alice. She's *my* cousin! My cousin Alice. Did you ever see
anybody so beautiful. So dainty. In all your life! With long golden
hair. And blue ribbons. She's my cousin! *My* cousin . . . Alice.
Look! Everybody just *LOOK*! That's *my* grandfather's horses
coming up the road. They're his horses . . . my grandfather.'

'My conscience, bairn!' Grandmother edged you out of her
road, and away from the window. 'You should know every tree
from this scullery window by heart! For I never did see anybody
who could stand so long. Just looking!'

That was about all you was good for, the Invalid Aunt confided
to Grandmother. It was high time, she insisted, that Ailsa found a
place for herself and that bairn! But, being man-mad, a bairn on
her hands would fair clip Ailsa's wings.

'Be quiet Edith!!' Grandmother admonished. 'It's your sister
you're speaking about.'

'Sister or no sister,' the Invalid Aunt said, 'Ailsa died to me a
long time ago.'

My Aunt Ailsa died to me
– Words of lament forming themselves in your mind –
A long long time ago
A dirge for a death, beyond your comprehension, singing in your
head.

'The *world*!' Grandmother announced, 'must surely be coming
to an end!' For, she informed you, this was only the second time
your Aunt Ailsa had bothered to write!

'If she's bothered to write,' the Invalid Aunt said, 'she must be
on the cadge for something or other. Either that, or she's lost her
job again. It's my opinion . . .'

'There's a time and a place for opinions,' Grandmother de-
clared, taking you by the hand into the scullery . . . 'Your Aunt
Ailsa is coming to see you the day,' she confided. 'She might have
some good news for you. So! Would it not be a good idea for you
to take a turn up the wood for some dry kindlers for the fire.'

Until Such Times had maybe arrived at last. The very thought of it fixed your feet to the cement of the scullery floor. With the voices from the kitchen rising and falling to the rise and fall of your own heart beats . . .

It was to be hoped, the Invalid Aunt was saying, that this chield would marry Ailsa this time. Though any man that did that had all the Invalid Aunt's sympathy! Either that or he must be a poor, simple creature that was of him!

Neither poor nor simple, Grandmother pointed out. A decent enough chield. A disabled war soldier.

That would fit the bill! the Invalid Aunt maintained. Knowing *Ailsa*, she would have her eye on his bit pension! And lucky to get that! Better women than Ailsa had never even got the *chance* of a man! It was the Invalid Aunt's opinion that Ailsa had never 'let on' about the bairn.

O but she did! Grandmother confirmed. She said in her letter that she was bringing him to see the bairn.

And that, the Invalid Aunt concluded, would be enough to put any man clean off! Unless of course, it was somebody they didn't know.

'We know of him,' Grandmother admitted. 'Summers. Dod Summers. His father's got that croft down by the railway.'

'I'm with you now!' The Invalid Aunt's voice shrilled out in triumph. 'Peg Leg Summers.' So that's who she's gotten. Old Peg Leg Summers. And he's got no pension. He shouldn't have been in the war in the first place. Well, well! Even I can mind on him! He used to go clop, clop, cloppin round the mart on a Friday!'

'Listen now,' Grandmother urged you. 'When your Aunt Ailsa comes the day, she'll maybe be bringing somebody with her . . .'

'She wouldn't!' you protested. 'I know she wouldn't. My Aunt Ailsa never *would*!'

'Good grief, bairn! What ails you?'

'What on earth are you on about?' Grandmother insisted, puzzled by your distress.

'My Aunt Ailsa. She wouldn't. She'd *never* marry a man with a wooden leg!'

'*Listening* again!' The Invalid Aunt snorted. 'Lugs cocking at the key hole!'

'Look a here. Just you look a here, now,' Grandmother said, easing you down on your stool by the door. 'A wooden leg's nothing. Nothing at all just. Many a brave man has a wooden leg. You like biding with your Aunt Alice,' she reminded you. 'Who has been making sore lament to get back to her Aunt Ailsa? Well then! You'll be happier with your Aunt Ailsa than you've been here. And fine you know that . . .'

'I wish to God she'd stop blubbering,' the Invalid Aunt complained. 'She should be thankful that somebody's willing to give her a home!'

'Now, listen, bairn, just you go and wash your face,' Grandmother suggested. 'And put on a clean pinny. You want to look your best to meet your Aunt Ailsa. But, first things first. I'll away to the well for some fresh water. You can follow on with the little pail.'

'Are you still blubbering there.' The Invalid Aunt's voice, battening itself against your hearing, was powerless to reach the horror of your imagination. 'You heard your Grandmother! You could at least obey her. But no faith you! Obedience would be some much to expect! *My*! But you're stubborn! Just like Ailsa. The living spit of the mother of you . . .'

'She's my Aunt Ailsa,' you said, protective of a relationship that was acceptable. 'She's my Aunt Ailsa. . . . She's not my *mother*!' The implication of the Invalid Aunt's words had penetrated at last, sending you hurtling towards her bed chair. 'She's my Aunt Ailsa!' Grasping the aunt by the shoulders, you tried to shake her into understanding. *My mother* is ladies I cut out from pictures in books. Ladies I pick out passing in the street! You know fine she's not my mother! You're just saying that because . . . because you're ugly! And you smell terrible! You're just a *fucker*!

. . . It wasn't *me* that swore, Grandfather. It wasn't me . . .

'My Aunt Ailsa's coming!' you shouted to Grandmother, bent over the well at the edge of the wood. 'She's all by herself. She wouldn't. I knew she wouldn't. Marry a man with a wooden leg!'

'I doubt you're right,' Grandmother agreed, as you stood together watching Aunt Ailsa coming up the track. 'Ah well!' she sighed, 'maybe it's all for the best. Who knows! Who can tell! You'd better run on and meet her, then. You haven't even washed your face!' Grandmother admonished. 'Nor changed your pinny! Whatever keepit you so long?'

'It was Edith,' you told Grandmother. 'I think the heart took her. She was making that funny noise.'

'Heaven above! O good grief.' The water from the pail that Grandmother dropped swirling round your feet.

'I didn't touch her medicine bottles!' you reassured her retreating figure. 'I didn't *touch* them!'

Good Friday

For more than a year now you had made a bee-line, first thing every morning, to the only window that looked down on the outside world.

A vigil shared with Miss Henly, at the opposite side of the window. The lines of demarcation were clearly defined. Neither intruded on the other's vision. Miss Henly spoke seldom but laughed often. Great gusts of laughter, that caught the ward up in the force of its gale. And left it quivering in the calm of the aftermath.

The turbanned women in the Co-op dairy across from the window were already pulling down the shining levers of their bottling machines. Raising their heads now and again, to gaze across into your world. Waving frantically, when they caught a glimpse of you. The way they might wave to an infant in a pram. Emphasising their presence.

You never waved back. You weren't a daftie. Acute neurasthenia. That was all that ailed you. It had no symptoms. At least, none you yourself recognised. Except when the passing of time took hold of you like a terror. And hurry clutched at you like a panic.

'*When?*' you would burst out, the instant the doctor got himself through the ward door. '*When* will I get *out?*'

When becoming timeless. Balanced in the doctor's long, silent calculation.

'When?'

'When you stop wringing your hands.'

You weren't even aware that you had been wringing your hands.

The groups of young office girls were making their way through the back gate now. Remembering also. Looking up towards the window.

'Do you see that girl? Miss Henly's query was directed to nobody in particular. But you responded. Without curiosity. Unable to distinguish the individual, amongst the faces, cast up like foam bells in a whirlpool.

'Do you know her, then?'

'Not in this life,' Miss Henly admitted. 'But I have known her. Somewhere. Sometime.'

That was the summer the swallows deserted you. Silently. Suddenly. As if you had betrayed them. It was *les hirondelles* out of a book of poetry the dominie had given you, that lay battered out on the tiles of the Co-op dairy. Basking like kittens in the sun. Secret birds. Exotic. Everybody else thought they were just swallows.

Light as a butterfly, the hand on your arm. But bone and sinew knew the touch of the fragile, tormented partner of your daily walk.

'He's at my neck, again! That man! My poor neck. Nip nip nippin' awa!'

'He'll go away soon,' you console. The pain in the hallucinated eyes was real enough. 'He won't come on our walk today!' you insist.

For yourself got wearied whiles of the third, invisible tormentor, who so often thrust himself on your company. Brief moment of ease, bringing lucid recollection.

'O lassie. The milk. And cheese. And fine sweet crowdie.'

The young girl, your own age, has taken up her day-long stance by the ward door. Ready to hurl herself on the first man who enters. Whether it is the chief medical superintendent, or the clock winder.

Madge. Her hand engloved in a yellow duster, is beginning to weave her way round the ward. Dusting the bed rails. A task unending. Set upon her by Hercules.

All words uttered in Madge's hearing become relevant. Essential. Stripped down to ballad bare bones. Only when the ward is wordless does Madge infringe on copyright. And lands you with herself, on Mormon Braes.

> Where heather grows
> Where oft-times I've been cheerie

You could avoid such a fate. You could rush to the old gramophone one of the nurses gave you, and put on the two sides of your only record. But usage has blunted it. Time has scarred it, and the heather on Mormon Braes never lost its bloom.

The knitting needles began to click through the ward. The old women, their pale tongues cleaving their chins in their absorption, sat knitting furiously against time. Pink socks for male patients.

Not for you such altruism. The ancient craftswomen, skilled in the cunning art of turning the heel. Could never show you how. Or explain such intricacies.

> No wise man utters what he only knows.
> Certainty in an uncertain world
> Is far too firm a treasure
> Wise man goes warily
> Jealously guarding
> His small particular knowledge

The nurses either didn't know how, or hadn't got time. And so your sock had gone far beyond human dimensions, in a year of weaving. Fit only for the seven-leagued legs of some footless giant. Its immensity bewildering the ancient craftswomen, and amusing the nurses.

Penelope? Athene?, aware of the futility of her task, has utterly abandoned it.

The telephone, beginning to ring through the ward, demanded instant concentration. For it never rang, but it rang for you. Even silent, cradled in its own shining aura of black magic, it never lost potential power. Some day. One day, it would ring for you.

And, although you could never visualise who the caller might be, you stood alert, always. Waiting for the summons. Strangely unprepared for it when it came.

Ginny. Your old china. Linked arm-in-arm with her new china, Meg. Giggling together at the uniqueness of their surrounding, and at their own temerity. They crowded your small austere room. It was never meant for company. It was the great confessional. Within its dark sleepless hours you made abject acknowledgement of the waste of your days. Strange noises usurped the small room. And crept about it. Shod with caution.

'You dinna *look* different!' Ginny had said, scrutinising your face. 'You dinna *look* daft!' she had concluded. Almost as if her finding had disappointed her. It was your gear that finally lived up to Ginny's horrific expectations. Your long grey flannel frock. And thick pink knitted stockings. It must have been the sight of the latter that impelled Ginny to urge you to:

'Beat it! Make a run for it! Scarper!'

No fate in all the world, it seemed to Ginny, garbed out in her black fishnets, could be worse than having to wear stockings that looked like her 'faither's combinations'.

There were no bars on the window, Ginny noticed. There was nothing to prevent you escaping.

'Dead easy,' Ginny said. Until she tried to raise the window herself!

Convinced at last that she could only leave you to your fate, combinations and all, Ginny had rushed into her next enthusiasm. 'The fella at the gate! The bloke that let us in! Mustard! A real sheik! Was he no, Meg?'

To which fact Meg had giggled her confirmation.

'*She* wadna mind a knockie doon to him!' Ginny claimed. 'You must have seen him,' she insisted. 'If not, Hen, you must have gone blind. As well as daft!'

Maybe Ginny was right. You had blinded yourself to all the outside workers, encountered on the long, crocodile walks.

They would come back to see you, again, Ginny had vowed. 'Sure we will, Meg. Sure we'll come back!'

Your heart accepted the momentary sincerity of the promise. But your mind knew that if Ginny ever did come back, it would be for another dekko of . . . the fella at the gate.

The ward door clanked open. Jean, massive behind the laundry trolley, pushed it towards the linen cupboard. In every institution in the land, you will find Jean. Hardworking, trustworthy. Too long inside to ever want to go outside. A boon, and a burden to the nurses. Nearly always a burden to her fellow-patients. Not that Jean ever considered herself a patient.

Still. It was from Jean that you learned most of the hospital's routine and its precedents. And most of what you had learned was depressing. She always seemed to get some kind of vicarious pleasure from your reactions to her adverse prophecies, which you knew were but the truth.

You would never, according to Jean, get out. You needed to have somebody to sign for you. Be responsible for you, like. That's why she herself had been here for over thirty years. Nobody to sign for her.

Puffing with the importance of having stacked all the laundry away, Jean plumped herself down on the bed nearest the window. She was, she said casually, thinking of having her tea out in the tea room in the grounds. But not until 'they' had passed. The senior doctor and the students were on their rounds. On their way here. She'd passed them in the north corridor.

The information sent you scurrying from the window to sit down on the bed with Jean. The doctor couldn't see your legs trembling when you sat down.

You might, you confided to Jean, ask the doctor today, if you could get ground parole. And go to the tea room.

'Not a chance!' Jean assured you. 'Not a hope! Because,' she confided in a conspiratorial whisper, 'young girls never get it. With all the bushes. And the gardener's boys!'

Madge had caught the relevant words, and began putting them together, in her ballad for the day:

> With the gardener's boys!
> With the gardener's boys!

She had just got it sorted out to her liking, when 'they' unlocked the door. Slipping on her cuffs, Charge Nurse advanced to meet them.

> In the bushes
> With the gardener's boys
> With the gardener's boys

At a passing signal from Charge Nurse, a junior removed the songstress to the kitchen. At another, two nurses untangled the young girl who had got herself enmeshed in the group of students. Miss Henly deserted the window, and laughingly pushed her way past the group, and out of focus. Caught unawares, but never unready, Jean leapt from the bed, and advanced to meet the group. Chiding the senior doctor with a familiarity which both horrified and impressed you.

'You haven't been to see me for ages! Dr Main!'

'Sorry about that, Jean. But . . .'

Charge Nurse cut short the doctor's apologies with a look. And a command.

'There's sluicing to be done, Jean! Have you forgotten?'

'And how are you this morning?'

The other walking patients had disappeared. It was you the doctor was speaking to.

'I'm fine,' you told him. Searching his face as closely as he searched yours. For this, according to Jean, was the doctor who held the keys to outside.

You could feel the sweat gathering at the roots of your hair, and beginning to trickle down your face. But you remembered not to wring your hands. And your feet, clamped firmly down on the wooden floor, kept your legs from shaking.

'I'm just fine,' you repeated. To make quite sure he had heard the first time. 'Just fine.'

The ward had become itself, again. Each of you took up your self-appointed stances. Friday. You remembered. A good day, Friday. Fish for dinner. And plum duff. Good Friday.

Senior Nurse's weekend off. Freedom. A flush of anticipation all over her. Flicking her cuffs in one hand. Rattling her keys in the other, in an impatience for the clock to strike twelve. Time had truly made you its numbering clock. You could have written out the off-duty lists yourself. But its chimes still startled you.

Rattling her keys aloft, in a final gesture of farewell, Senior Nurse admonished us cheerfully.

'Behave yourselves now, till I get back! Don't do anything I wouldn't do!'

And, uninhibited by the absence of Charge Nurse, her long, blackclad legs skated the whole length of the polished floor. Pausing to chuck Madge under the chin, she turned at the ward door, and bending down on one knee, beseeched of her watchful, wordless audience.

'Why do men adore me?'

And disappeared in a clang of doors and a flurry of white.

The ward absorbed her disappearance in complete silence. But quivered still, in the aura of her exhilaration.

You began to circle with the bed patients' trays. Madge, beginning to dust the bed rails again, took off once more for Mormon Braes.

> I'll nae go intae mourning
> I'll nae put on my gown of green
> For my true love ne'er returning

Fully in voice now, she ceased dusting. And you ceased circling to join in, and give the ballad the crescendo it deserved.

> Ye Mormon Braes
> Where heather grows
> Where oft-times I've been cheerie . . .

The ward door clanged open. Charge Nurse stood on its threshold. Static. Knowing, no doubt, that the 'artists' – like all true artists – could not stop in the middle of a performance, listened until we reached a shaky falsetto close:

> Fare ye weel ye Mormon Braes
> It was there I lost my dearie

'You!' It was you Charge Nurse spoke to. 'Can get down off Mormon Braes right now! And come and have a bath!'

A bath! At dinner-time! On a Friday!

Saturday was bath night!

'A bath!' Charge Nurse repeated. 'Right now!'

It was only when you got into the bathroom that Charge Nurse told you. 'You're getting out! They're waiting for you round at the front. I didn't want you to know till the last minute! You would have got over-excited. And that would have been that!'

You couldn't be getting out. No place to go. No one to go to.

'You're going to your domicile,' Charge Nurse said. 'To the Highlands. The place where you were born. To work on a croft in the hills. It will do more for you than this has done. Besides,' she insisted, 'I never want to see your face here again!'

It was only when you saw your own clothes folded on a chair by the bath, that reality hit you.

'Nurse!' Charge Nurse flung open the bathroom door, and shouted down the ward: 'Nurse! Bring a sheet for this daft lassie. to cry into. She's crying here. Because we're letting her *out*!'

Life Model

They almost knocked her flat on her face. The young students bounding up the steps of St Martin's School for Art. But then she was not so steady on her legs now, and finding stairs harder to climb. You slowed down a bit when you had crossed seventy.

'Do you know how old I am?' she would sometimes ask, in a hoarse, conspiratorial whisper, of the young students, who brought her coffee up to the cubicle, to save her legs the long trudge down to the cafeteria.

It always disappointed her that they never said, as she half hoped they *would* say,

'You don't *look* seventy-two!'

'You can't be!'

They would say instead: 'Nobody could hold a standing pose for a whole day. Not at seventy-two!'

But she *could*. And she did.

Dear God . . . she remembered, as she stood 'getting her breath' . . . *thank* you for making me strong enough to hold a standing pose. But if I *do* get a booking today, make it be just portrait or costume. So that I can just sit down and take the weight off my legs . . .

If it be *your* will, she added hastily. For although she had established a close, 'on speaking terms' relationship with God over the years, nobody ever got close enough to dictate *their* terms to *Him* . . .

Her relationship with God had started all those years ago. When she had stepped out from behind her curtain for the very first time. Naked and revealed to a blur of faces.

It was her legs that had begun to give way, before extending to a convulsion of her whole body. With sweat gathering in substance and momentum, till it dropped from her like rain, to gather in pools round her bare feet.

'Our Father . . .' she had repeated to herself, her mind grasping for something to hold on to, until her body had eased itself down into stillness again, under the intensity of her repetition: ' . . . Our Father'.

And, in all the years since, she had never trembled, sweated, or felt ashamed.

' – Hallowed be Thy name . . .'

What job satisfaction can you ever get out of being an artist's model, the social security lady was always asking.

And Nella had never been able to put it into words. Not even to herself.

Maybe . . . maybe the social security lady was right. It wasn't like a 'job'. It was something different . . .

Something you became completely involved in. Something you took out with you from behind your curtain. You could never tell what it was. But you always knew when you had taken it.

You knew by the silence that fell over the students, broken by their hurried rush to capture it. By the blankness on their faces when the tutor's voice brought the strange, trance-like involvement to an end.

– Thank you, model. Rest now . . .

'It isn't as if modelling was *real* work', the social security lady was always insisting . . .

'*Real* work,' Nella would always protest. 'It's the *hardest* work in the world. The easiest pose is agony after the first twenty minutes. Even just sitting for portrait. Your hip bones start growing into the chair. And the chair don't want them. And the battle between you is on!'

The ultimate revenge of inanimate things. Nella knew all about *that*. But had no words to describe it to the social security lady . . .

Nella!

A voice rang in her ears. And a hand grasped her shoulder. Names sometimes eluded her, faces seldom. Professor of Fine Arts now . . . But a student in the distant days of her 'block bookings', Always a gentleman, she remembered. *Still* a gentleman. Still bought her a coffee along with his own – whenever he saw her in the cafeteria.

'What is the *secret* of your stillness, Nella?' he had once asked her. 'I never had a model who could stand so long. So *still* as you.'

'The Lord's Prayer,' she had told him, grinning, her grin widening as the confusion on his face increased. 'Just the Lord's Prayer. Three times at a very slow pace. And I knew my hour was up. I never had to look at the clock!'

'I could draw Nella blindfold,' he was saying to the students gathering up behind him. 'I am more familiar with Nella's contours than I am with the map of England.'

Someone who *really* knew. Someone who remembered, from her first young years as 'The Pocket Venus' of St Martins, to her middle years as their 'Rubens Model', to her decline, when her body was dissolving down into nothingness. And she had become a face. A '*head*' for portrait. 'Plantaganet' they said. Something to do with history.

'Have you got a booking, Nella?' She shook her head.

'I was passing. I just popped in. On the off chance . . .'

'The thing is . . .' he hesitated, ' . . . the thing is . . .'

She wished she could give him the words he was searching for. She *knew* them. Young models coming up. New faces –

'I've booked a model for today. But –'

He turned, as if in appeal, to the students –

'We *could* use *two* models. Just for old time's sake . . .'

The gesture warmed her heart. But her mind rejected it. She had found the answer for the social security lady. She knew at *last* what job satisfaction meant.

'I got the chance of a booking, the other day . . .' she would say to the social security lady. 'They still *remember* me, you see! But it was for old time's sake. And I refused it – for old time's sake!'

Road of No Return

I found the road because I expected to find it. It was not easy, after forty years. And, as I had searched for it through memory's eyes, I was to discover that memory was misleading.

Had I so forgotten summers, then? Wind-blown anemones and stars of Bethlehem, that flitted white and furtive amongst the bracken? Or was it just that spring had out-blossomed all the other seasons of my mind?

'You must not pluck the primroses on the Sabbath,' my Aunt Teenac had commanded haltingly. Searching for 'the English' that could convey the strength of her Gaelic commandment

'You must not . . .'

Yet she was a *good* woman, my Aunt Teenac. Everybody on the hill said she was. She subscribed to Dr Barnardo's Homes every Christmas. 'And never told a living soul about it,' they all said.

How then, did they all know?

I had never considered this contradiction till now. Yet she was still a good woman. Even my adult cynicism was forced to admit *that*. At least she was moved to 'subscribe', something that has never happened to me.

But she was adamant about the primroses. And I never plucked them. Somewhere, somewhen, though, my spirit must have defied her embargo, and gone flying down that hill, stumbling into that wood, and tearing and gathering unto itself all the primroses it could ever contain, for I still hold within my nostrils their faint and passing sweetness. And my fingers still know the rough and hairy texture of their leaves.

Perhaps it was not as far-fetched as all that. It may be that I plucked them on the Friday nights of spring, when we all raced down the hill to meet Neil, the grocer's van. For our hill was far too steep for his van to come up to us.

I doubt it, though. I had other things on my mind! I doubt too, if I ever was 'beautiful'. But I know for certain that I felt 'beautiful', on those far off Friday nights. My hair brushed till my scalp ached, with Aunt Teenac grumbling in the background.

'Yourself and that little bit of hair that's on you! And you haven't even boiled the rooshacs for the hens, yet.' And my legs, which *were* 'good', aching within the tightness of my garters, so that not one wrinkle should show on my stockings. My skirt as short as Aunt Teenac would allow. And hitched up that little bit shorter the moment the house was out of sight.

'*You* will come to a Bad End,' Aunt Teenac had always prophesied.

She didn't live long enough to know that I didn't. But I sometimes wonder if the knowing would have pleased her. She liked her prophecies to be proved correct. Did my Aunt Teenac.

It may be that it was but lack of opportunity on my part that disrupted her prophecies! But certain it was that my hair glinted, my stockings stayed taut, my whole being glowed in anticipation of a chance encounter with one person and one person only. 'The Boxer'. So named, not so much for the power behind his fists, as for the dexterity of his fingers on the keys of the melodeon.

> And time and tide
> Shall be nae mair.
> O gin I were the Baron's heir.
> Lassie, I was lo'e Thee

He played for his own pleasure, and was possibly almost unaware of my existence. But since all music and any melody is taken personally, and to heart, when one is sixteen, it was still a potential 'baroness' who puzzled over and deciphered Aunt Teenac's grocery list, with Neil, the vanman, knowing, if it *was* 'half a stone sugar' she wanted, it would still not be too much sweetness for so sweet a world. But yet aware that 'a quarter stone of sugar' would be lighter to carry up the hill.

The shed where 'the Boxer' played on those spring Fridays still stood at the foot of the hill. Emitting a sense of timelessness. A timelessness dispelled the moment I reached the top of the hill. For I missed something I could put no name upon. And stood for a long time, wondering what it was.

It had never been a land that sang with colour, except in late autumn. Hard to tell then whether it was the heather, or the red rocks that so assailed the skies, and made the loudest impact. At all other times it was a grey land, mottled with silver. Small burns leaping over the dun stones, and rushing down through the birch trees. Yet it had always 'smouldered' behind its greyness. The smoke of its hidden fires would catch at your throat, and envelop you forever. Even at your desk in school, ignorant of where 'the trade winds' blew. Or why they blew at all. You would hide your head between your arms, and your ignorance would find its comfort in the warm, peaty smell of your jersey's sleeves. There was no peat-reek now. The houses scattered on the slopes stood with heart-remembered names. Achullen. Balbec. Tullorach. Balmore. But you had now become aware that they were empty. Staring sightless down over Loch Ness. Blind to the tourists' caravans, and the scientific ships, searching for a monster that *they* had never glimpsed in all their window-wide and watchful years.

The school was deserted, too. But, rushing down the wind, I could hear a prayer in a Glasgow accent.

'"*Butter*!" Bu – *tt* – er! Please let me remember to say "bu*tt*er." *Not* "bu'r." Or I'll get the strap!'

'My' house was not deserted though. It was burnt to the ground. But how? And when? There was no enlightening sermon in the charred and silent stones surrounding it. No book of explanation in the running brooks that passed it. And the only

immediacy, the long silent voice of Aunt Teenac, urging me to 'go
west to the burn for water' and 'east to the barn for straw'.

The clump of wallflowers that straggled amongst the debris
could have been those of my memory, growing under the scullery
window. A face-length away, on summer mornings.

> That smelt so heavenly sweet.
> The senses *ached* at thee

Only of the rhubarb could I be sure. Itself grotesque. A great
umbrella of green. Sheltering and towering above the fence that
had once contained it. Outwith and far beyond Aunt Teenac's
anguished lament.

'Ochone, ochone. I forgot to put the ginger for the rhubarb
down on my list.'

Gone too was all trace of the sacred stairs that ascended up to
Uncle Ian's bedroom. Even after his once-a-year celebration of the
sale of his sheep, Uncle Ian would still 'remember his Maker',
with his alarm clock in his hand, kneeling on the stairs, either
through sheer inability to mount them, or genuine Christian
fervour. And because he was not only a good man, but a kindly
man as well, I give him the benefit of the doubt – he would pray in
Gaelic, till morning came. Fortified, I like to think, to meet Aunt
Teenac's tightfaced disapproval. 'What a man that's in it. And
what will the neighbours be thinking of it all?'

I was not a nice child. I stood realising that.

'Uncle Ian was drunk, last night', I would announce to all with
whom I came in contact. Aware for once that I had something to
tell, important enough for them to *listen* to!

'As drunk as a tinker. Aunt Teenac was just furious!'

Given the chance again, I would hug Uncle Ian's rare but
intense 'remisses' to my heart. Or confide them only to laughter-
lifted things, like the flying clouds and the rushing wind. And I
would put it differently. Clothing it with the words and tune of
Uncle Ian's favourite psalm.

When Zion's bondage God turned back.
As men that dreamed were we.
Then filled with laughter was our mouth.
Our tongues with melody

It was when I was coming down the hill, that I met the new inhabitant going up. Retired there, from Inverness. Cars could easily go up the hill now, he assured me. His own was being serviced at the moment. Yes. Television reception was quite good. The croft he had converted had all 'mod cons' now. Soon all the crofts would be 'snapped up.' Cheaper in the long run than all the caravans lining the lochside, there. An ideal place for retirement. With air like this. And scenery second to none.

No one *ever* 'retired' on the hill, my mind protested. They just died when their work was done. But he was right. Everything he said was reasonable so there was no logic for my resentment. But resentment was within me. Tangible and hard as a lump I could have put my hand on, and squeezed.

No. He hadn't known any of the former inhabitants. The crofts had been empty for a long time. Oh there was one. An old boy, turned tramp, who lived at the foot of the hill in an old hut. Found dead there from exposure last winter. Nothing at all in his hut except some old coats.

'And a melodeon,' I heard myself confirming.

If there ever *was* a melodeon, the stranger was sure it would have been sold 'for drink' long since. Everything had gone for drink. Even his social security money. Had I known the man, then?

I wasn't sure. It could have been another man I had known.

As I passed the hut at the foot of the hill I knew that I *never* would be sure. Never till

time and tide shall be nae mair
Gin I were the Baron's heir
O Lassie . . .

Dear Edith . . .

The Warden of Anson House – a Home for Elderly Indigent Ladies – slammed the telephone down.

'We'd best get our skates on. A new resident's coming,' she snapped to her trainie assistant. 'Struth!' she grumbled, as she led the way upstairs. 'They hardly give the old dears time to die before they pop another into their place!'

'This lot will take some clearing out,' her assistant reflected as they stood staring round the recently vacated bed-sitting-room. 'Books! Must be hundreds of them! Old Cresswell could never have read all this lot!'

'She reckoned she did.' The Warden automatically flicked her hand across the bookshelves in her compulsive search for dust. 'Nothing better to do, I suppose. And time to do it in.'

'She wasn't a bad old stick,' the assistant ventured.

'We've had worse,' the Warden conceded.

'No next of kin, had she?'

'Not that I know of. And there was no mention on her admission sheet. There was' – the Warden straightened herself up from stripping the bed – 'some woman she'd shared a flat with for years . . . what was her name again? *I* ought to know, didn't I? It'll come to me . . . it always does. when you're not thinking about it . . . *Edith*! I knew it would come! It was when Edith died that old Cresswell came here. Same year as myself. And that's ten years since! "My friend Edith", on and on, as if Edith was still alive! Gave me a bit of a turn at first, being new to the work . . . "I must write to my friend Edith".'

'And did she? Write, I mean.'

'If she did,' the Warden said, '*I* never saw a letter go out from old Cresswell. Nor come in for her either.'

'I suppose they get like that, muddled . . .'

'Confused.' The Warden supplied the correct 'medical' term before bending again to strip the bed.

'Dear Edith,

The horse chestnut tree in front of my window is in full bloom now. It set me thinking about you, took me back, back to that Sunday. We had just come out from the cemetery, our usual afternoon visit. No that we had either kith or kin buried there, but as you always said since we would be longer there than anywhere else on earth, we might as well get accustomed to the place. Maybe, I don't know, maybe that was still on your mind when we sat in our usual seat in the park. The wind must have been beginning to rise, the red petals of the horse chestnut trees were fluttering down all round us, I started to play a little game – closing my eyes then opening them to see if any of the petals had landed on my shoes. "Don't be so childish!" you said. "Pay attention to what I am saying! When we come to be a burden to others, we will find our *own* way out . . ." That was when we put our plan into operation. Setting aside a few of our Seconal pills out of each monthly prescription. Better, you explained, to go sleepless for a few nights, than to be unprepared *if* . . .'

'Didn't you hear me knocking, Miss Cresswell! Forgot to put your hearing aid in *again* . . .'

'Sorry, Miss Ainslie, I was just finishing off a letter to –'

'Not feeling poorly again are you, dear?'

'No – thank you – I was just . . .'

'Anyhow! Miss Cresswell, I just popped in to tell you the Committee Ladies have arrived to take us out for a little "run". I thought you might like –'

'Thank you, Miss Ainslie. Kind of you to bother, but I . . .'

'Don't feel *up* to it? Between *ourselves*, Miss Cresswell, neither do *I*. Thing is, thing is dear, the Ladies *expect* us to go. To show willing. They get a bit tetchy if –'

'Yes, I see. Very well, I'll just finish off my letter.'

'Oh, Edith, I have forgotten what privacy is like. The Committee Ladies have swooped down on us again . . .'

'Ah! Miss Cresswell! Come to join us for a little "spin". That's a girl! Just the day for it. How about you, Miss Miller-Browne. Won't you join us today? Do you a world of good!'

'No, thank you! If *I* could go anywhere at all, with one foot in a caliper, and the other in the grave, I would gather up my skirts and get myself out of here – in a very rapid manner!'

'I know, Edith, I know I should be grateful for all that the Committee Ladies try to do for us, it's just, I get so tired of *having* to feel grateful. I was cajoled into going for a run. Helped and heaved into the car, we got stuck in a traffic jam on the way back, I found it so hard to contain myself. As you know, I always did suffer from a weak bladder . . .

'Miss Miller-Browne refused as usual, to be cajoled. She always reminds me of you. She has such courage.'

'*Bloody-minded*! That's what *I* call Miller-Browne,' the Warden confided to her assistant, as they stood unwiring the flowers sent in from the crematorium. 'Uncooperative! Never leaves the house. Scared we get a minute to ourselves – anti-social!'

'To put our feet up,' the assistant agreed. 'This lot' she reflected, stripping the bottom leaves from the chrysanthemums, 'must have cost a bomb!'

'*Waste*!' the Warden agreed. 'Even the *dead* don't get the good of them. Not at the crematorium!'

'A rose tree now,' her assistant said. 'That's a different thing!

You can plant that in the Vale of Rest. That's what *we* did when our Aunt Freda got cremated . . . we didn't bother with *flowers*!'

'Flowers from the dead to the dying. According to Miss Ainslie, who overheard as usual . . . I wondered what *you* would make of that, Edith . . .

  'I tried to imagine, to hear you, "a natural and thoughtful gesture on the part of the dead," something like that, maybe? I chose some freesias. They seemed less death-like than the other flowers. I put them into that small green vase you gave me on a birthday . . .

  '"Green," you said, "will never clash with flowers of any hue. Which is why nature is so prodigal of its use."'

  'What are your beads?'

  '"Green glass, goblin . . ."'

  'Remember? Strange isn't it? I can remember long ago things, they just pop into my head of their *own* accord.

> 'They are brighter than stars
> Brighter than water
> Better than voices of winds that sing
> Better than any man's fair daughter
> . . . your green glass beads . . .

  'It's the little every day things which I *ought* to remember, that sometimes elude me. And makes the Warden annoyed with me . . .'

  '*Laundry*! Miss Cresswell. Don't forget your laundry again! Bring it down when you come to supper. Van collects first thing in the morning – *laundry*, I said!'

  'Yes, yes, Warden. It's my hearing-aid. The battery's finished and I . . . forgot.'

  'Struth!' The Warden grumbled to her assistant as they pre-pared supper. 'They do go on and on. Demanding. Always demanding. Nothing ever seems to be enough for them. Almost as if' – she paused, struggling to find words to fit her thought, 'as if old age entitled them to everything . . . owed them. "I need a new hearing aid, Warden!" "I need a new bottom set. My lower dentures are slipping!" "I need a new Zimmer. This one's too high for me now!" And you can't tell them that their gums are shrinking. Their bodies are shrinking. They don't want to know! They don't even listen to Dr Crombie when he tells them that he hasn't got a cure for old age! You'll learn!' she assured her assistant. 'If you stick this job long enough!'

'It'll come to us all, I suppose,' the assistant said, 'if we live that long!'

'God forbid we should!' the Warden snapped. 'And don't forget to put out the mustard pot tonight!'

'*Mustard*! With *fish*, warden? It's fish tonight!'

'With *everything*!' the Warden confirmed. 'Mustard with everything! Just goes to show,' she reflected. '"A *bland* diet, Warden." Committee always insisting on a "bland diet". They want to cook *here* for a week! You keep your ears cocked to the serving hatch,' she advised her assistant, 'and you'll hear what the old ones think of blancmange, tapioca, semolina. *No*!' she asserted. 'They like a good old fry-up. And I don't blame them for *that*! A bit of "taste". I reckon it don't matter much what you eat when you're on the last lap. It's just the *mustard* I can't get over!'

'Maybe,' her assistant suggested 'they were used to it when they were young.'

'I don't know about *that*!' the Warden admitted. 'I'd just like a word in the geriatric dietician's ears!'

'. . . I had intended to look through my book shelves in the hope of coming across one book that I haven't yet read. The mobile library comes, of course. But the choice is limited. That was *before* supper. *After* supper, Edith, I seldom feel in the mood to do anything at all. I, thankfully, cannot grumble about my health, it is reasonably good, but when we all gather together at meals, the main topic of conversation is aches and pains. By the time the meal is over, I feel that I suffer from every ill that afflicts man, as if the symptoms of the others have invaded me. What affects me, Edith, what frightens me most, is the anticipation with which what I can only describe as "medical days" are looked forward to. And when the unexpected happens, as it sometimes does – "repeat prescriptions" a day late in arriving, chiropodist's visit postponed, ambulance arriving half an hour late for the checkups – the blank that falls down on the day is filled with complaint. For the "medical days" have become the highlights of our weeks, of our existence.

'The seasons are brought in to us. Miss Ainslie told me that she heard the Warden discussing the Harvest Festival . . .'

'Miss Cresswell! The Vicar!'

'. . . He's arrived, dear. *And* Church Sister – thought I'd better let you know. We're all getting together in the dining-room . . .'

'. . . And we look forward,' the Vicar was saying, 'to having those amongst you who are able to do so, joining us in our Harvest Home Service on Sunday morning.'

'We will, of course,' Church Sister reminded the Vicar, 'provide transport for those who are not quite so able. I have the list here. Miss Brecon, Miss Harris, Mrs Wade, Miss Miller-Browne . . .'

'Wait for it!' the Warden whispered to her assistant, as they stood together, peeping through the half-closed serving hatch. 'Miss Miller-Browne won't. She never does!'

'. . . Miss Miller-Browne,' the Church Sister was persuading 'you'll try to make the effort this year, won't you?'

'I have told you *before*! I have no truck with the Church since I was a child, and *then* under compulsion. But I *do* know the Bible! "Remember thy Creator in the days of thy Youth . . ." I didn't do so then! And am most unlikely to do so in my old age!'

'I knew it,' the Warden triumphed. 'She is an old so-and-so, Miller-Browne. Just the same,' the Warden admitted reluctantly, 'she sticks to her guns. Look at her! Calliper or no calliper! She can't half move herself out of it when something annoys her.'

'. . . The altar looked beautiful this morning, surrounded by autumn. Sheaves of corn intertwined with tea roses. We used to think, you and I, Edith, that tea roses looked old. Older than other roses. Because you said, they had their roots in a civilisation far older than ours – India? China? Persia? I forget.

'The Girl Guides sang – did I tell you? We have been "adopted" by a Girl Guide. A nice child, mine. She came to have tea with me in my room. We talked and talked, but didn't communicate. The gap was too wide to be bridged by words . . . and yet today it seemed to be bridged in an almost miraculous way. The Vicar didn't announce this hymn, you see. The Girl Guides simply stood up, and the music seemed to swell out from nowhere . . . *your* hymn, Edith.

> 'Choose me in my golden time
> In my dear joys . . .
> Have part . . .
> For Thee the . . .
> Fullness of my prime
> The gladness . . .'

'*Singing*! Miss Cresswell! You *are* in good spirits! I just popped up dear, to let you know – tip you the *wink*! They've just brought in the Harvest Festival Offerings from the church, and remember what happened to *you* last Harvest Festival, Miss Cresswell! Only a few russets left by the time you came down to collect your share. Miss Brecon took the lion's share of the grapes! Said apples went for her dentures!'

'I don't mind, Miss Ainslie. *Truly*, I don't.'

'You *should* mind, Miss Cresswell. We're all entitled! Warden ought to supervise the share-out. I daresay after she gets her pick, it's devil take the hindmost!'

'I doubt that. Now Miss Ainslie, if you'll excuse me . . .'

'. . . And so, Edith, autumn was brought into us and piled high on the sideboard, a pyramid of colour. We could only stand looking at it, arrested by the intensity of the colour that confronted us. Apprehensive of putting out a hand towards it, lest it should tumble down at our touch. That moment and that mood passed, and *then* . . .!'

'*Ladies*! See what I mean?' the Warden flung over her shoulder to her assistant, as she flounced out of the kitchen into the dining-room.

'Ladies! There's surely enough here for all of you! The others like grapes, too, Miss Brecon!'

'Ladies?' the Warden sniffed, perching herself up on her stool beside the serving hatch again. 'I don't know . . . Better take your pick of what's left,' she suggested to her assistant. 'And there's not much of *that* now. Not after *that* lot's had a go.

'When I first came here' she reflected, 'ten long years since, the secretary who interviewed me for the job – a Miss Fenwick she was. Dead now – went on and on about "putting me fully in the picture". She said. "We don't accept 'God Blimmees' here", she told me. For a minute, I thought she meant *me*! And that I'd *had* the job! Till she went on to explain that they cared for women who had "seen better days", had "come down in the world". Sometimes,' the Warden sighed, 'I wish she wasn't dead. Fenwick, I mean. *I* could have told *her* something! There are ladies – and – *ladies*! And Brecon's not one. Nor Ainslie – '

'Miss Cresswell?' her assistant prompted.

'Cresswell?' the Warden considered the matter. 'She's not with us half the time, but she'll pass.'

'Miller-Browne?'

'She's the *real* thing. You can always tell!' the Warden claimed. 'She didn't go to their Harvest Service, but she didn't barge in here and grab all the grapes either!'

'. . . Christmas is almost upon us. How I dread it, Edith. Cards that come. Cards that go. A contest of cards. To see which of us can lay claim to the largest number of cards received, to prove something to ourselves? That we still have friends? Are still in touch with the world outside? That we still exist? Cards which will not herald the advent of this Christmas but testify to Christmas long past from well-wishers long dead. I realised this when Miss Ainslie invited me to her room to see "all her cards". I recognised the names of residents, now gone from us, I made no mention of my discovery to Miss Ainslie. Then gifts, no longer personal, from friend to friend, but public tokens of our continued existence. Without the small surprise that sharpened and sweetened our Christmas tides, Edith, or so I feel. You see, Edith . . .'

'*Yes*! *Yes*! Miss Ainslie, I heard you knocking . . . I'm just trying to . . .'

'An artificial tree this year, Miss Cresswell. I've just seen the Council men bring it in by the back door. Not the same as a *real* treat. Not the same thing at all! To save the Warden I suppose. Always complaing about the fir needles on the carpet! *Anything* to save herself work! I thought I'd pop up to remind you that we've got to go into the sitting-room before tea. The Committee Ladies are coming.'

'. . . to put you *all* in the picture!' Miss Sherwood, the Secretary announced, flicking through the lists of her Christmas agenda.

'You must,' Miss Ainslie invited her, 'pop in for a minute to see all my cards. More than last year!'

'Yes, yes. They do seem to mount up, don't they?' The Secretary acknowledged the invitation without accepting it, or lifting her eyes from her agenda.

'First of all!' she proclaimed, handing her lists over to her assistant and trusting to memory. 'The Ladies of St Saviour's have once again risen nobly to the occasion. And will provide *and* serve tea on Christmas Eve, as usual. Then our Girl Guides, carols on Christmas morning. The Vicar himself will be along after Morning Service.'

The applause which greeted this announcement, although appreciative, was modulated. For the old ladies knew the rote. They also knew what was what, and who was who.

'Then!' the Secretary continued, 'the Rotarians' – the applause which greeted this announcement put her slightly off her stroke – 'yes the Rotarians – always so generous in their giving – will be along.' Forgetful of when exactly the Rotarians would 'be along', the Secretary, grabbing the agenda out of her assistant's hand, began to flick wildly through its pages. 'So many bits and pieces,' she complained. 'Where *did* I put the Rotarians?'

'In your handbag?' her assistant suggested.

'Of course! The Rotarians,' she announced 'will be with us to hand out their gifts, just after lunch on Christmas Day.'

'You will pop in to see my cards?' Miss Ainslie reminded her.

'Another time, dear,' the Secretary assured her, before turning to assure the Warden. 'That's everything, Miss Watson, everything under control!'

'Everything under control!' the Warden snorted, when herself and her assistant reached the safety of their kitchen again. 'She forgets how they all collapse like burst balloons *after* Christmas! You won't see hair or hide of madam then! Not when all the viruses start going around. It's you and me that have to cope then! Strange thing,' she reflected, 'how the old dears always seem to be able to hang on like grim death till Christmas. After that' – the warden shrugged – 'they just seem to let go.'

'Nothing to look forward to?' the assistant suggested.

'Could be,' the Warden agreed. 'Could be. Or that they think they mightn't reach another Christmas.'

'. . . And everything was laid on, Edith. Christmas got smothered and wept to get out. But, again, the Girl Guides sang beautifully. Echoing for me, Christmas remembered. *Our* hymn. Always my favourite. Though I could never tell why. Not until you discovered the reason. "A poem," you said, "Christina Rossetti." I sang it silently. From beginning to end, with the Girl Guides. Yet, now, I cannot remember one word of it. That happens to me, sometimes. And it vexes me. Things that tremble on the edge of my mind. Eluding capture. Battering against my brain, for outlet. Tormenting me. As if I could never find release, till I find the words . . . in the bleak

> '*Midwinter*!
> Frosty winds made moan
> Earth . . .
> Lay hard as iron
> Water . . .
> *Like*
> . . . a stone . . .

'A ghost? No. Ghosts walk at midnight . . .'

'Miss Brecon! It's Miss Brecon, dear – ambulance has just come for her. Different when it comes for a check-up, but when it's for hospital . . .'

'That's the first of them!' the Warden announced to her assistant. 'And there's Ainslie, creeping around, spreading the Glad Tidings! Miss Ainslie!' she demanded. 'What are you hovering up there for! Keeping Miss Cresswell's door open. As if it isn't cold enough!

'Hospital always "gets" them,' she confided to her assistant.

'Frightened they never come out. But,' she admitted, 'better to happen in hospital. When it happens here, it really does affect them.'

'Wondering whose turn next!' her assistant supposed.

'. . . Miss Brecon was admitted to hospital three weeks ago. We have just heard from Warden that she died yesterday. It's when death occurs *here* that Warden doesn't discuss it with us. We are taken "out" by the back door then. As if that could conceal a fact. A virus, Warden said. It seems to be catching. Dr Comrie came this morning to Miss Miller-Browne and Miss Hardwick. I haven't been feeling too well myself. In spirit. I used to like my room, my books, and all the small momentoes of our life together, but now, Edith, now the walls of my room seem to crowd in on me, the momentoes to mock me. I feel like crashing them through the window. And pounding at the walls with my hands. I find myself wishing that I could dissolve with no trace left. I couldn't say so to the others, but I envied Miss Brecon her escape. I'm not afraid to die. But sometimes, Edith, sometimes I feel frightened to death . . .'

'That's that, then!' The Warden surveyed the empty bed-sitting-room.

'This junk,' her assistant asked, 'where does it go?'

'Basement still,' the Warden considered. 'Some of it might "come in" one day. You never know.'

'I didn't expect old Cresswell to go. Not sudden like that,' the assistant said. 'She wasn't ill. Not *properly* ill, I mean.'

'Heart! Her heart was always dicky! And old age. We all die of *that* through time.' The Warden stood considering a philosophy that had just struck her. 'Another thing!' she remembered resentfully. 'When Dr Comrie came to sign the death certificate – going for midnight, it was. And he doesn't like late calls. But what about *me*! I don't like late calls either! And I had to be there too! I was jittery, I always am when they go off, sudden. Nervous. You know what I mean. You open your mouth and let anything come out of it. "Old people are living longer now Doctor," I said. Just for something to say, when he was signing the death certificate. STRUTH! You would think that *I* had killed old Cresswell! "Old people are *lingering* longer!" he snapped, flung down the pen, and shot out the door. I felt as if my nose had bled! That's *it* then! Have you finished clearing out the chest of drawers?'

'Just about.'

'Good, I'll see to this lot.'

'Warden! Warden!' the assistant's voice halted the Warden at the door. 'Look at this!' she urged. 'Just take a look! Writing paper. Pages and pages! "Dear Edith . . ." Nothing else. Just "Dear Edith." What a waste of paper!'

'No wonder they're always crying out for writing paper,' the Warden snapped. 'Just to waste it!'

'I could,' her assistant suggested, 'I could just cut off the tops and the others could use up the rest of the paper.'

'You're welcome to the job! If you can find time to do it.'

'Warden! She *has* written something! On this page – "Dear Edith I have changed my mind. Not about my going. The reason for it has changed, other people have become a burden to me . . ."'

This Wasted Day

Day had slipped over her head. Forcing her way through the bramble bushes, she eased herself down in the ley of the dyke. Time now for a smoke, to recover from the weariness of a wasted day, before taking the long road back to the town.

> Tinkie Tinkie
> Tarry Bags . . .

The bairns, just let out of school, raced chanting past her, before riving in and out amongst the bushes in search of brambles.

> Lay your eggs
> Amang your Rags!

Long since inured to their mockery, she automatically whipped the cover off her basket, to check up on her 'swag'. A profitless day. Few blanks appeared in the precise rows of tape, elastic, safety-pins, needles, reels of cotton, so carefully set out, when morning was still early. But then, most days were profitless now. Wearying in their wastefulness. . . . WOOLWORTHS! *That* was what had tolled the knell of her livelihood. 'Cheaper,' country folk said. 'A better selection'. Closing their doors before she had time to whip the cover off her basket. Not that there were many country folk left now. Not *real* country folk. The rows of cottages once inhabited by her regular customers had now been taken over as week-end residences by folk from the town. New-fangled machinery had taken over from many of the farm workers. Like herself, they had outlived their era, had become out of step with the times that had replaced it.

Aki! The Paki!
His sackie
On his backie! . . .

The bairns had found a new target. She could hear them
shouting in the distance. 'God curse *you* too,' she muttered,
adding to their jibes, as the Indian 'tally man' whizzed whistling
past on his bicycle, his 'pack' slung across his shoulders. He and
his kind had also replaced her. For what *he* offered was not to be
found in the town – hand-painted cushion covers, rolls of silk,
brass falderals. All the same . . . The recollection warmed her, lit
up her eyes, as she watched him swerving his way through a
crowd of shouting bairns, his foot trailing behind him on the
ground. All the same . . . neither man, beast nor bairn would have
tried *that* with her in the days when she took to the road with her
'sheltie' and her 'float'. Spanking along it. Her whip cracking high
in the wind. Snapping in threat to anyone who dared to bar her
way.

Restored to good humour, she set about clearing out the bowl
of her clay pipe. Poking at it. Dunting it against her fist, prepara-
tory to the precise, careful ritual of 'filling up'. One good thing
about a clay pipe, she reflected, if you dropped it you didn't have
to bother picking it up. But she was careful of her clay pipe. Hard
to come by now. 'No demand for them,' according to the wife
in the tobacconist's shop. Advising her to 'try the toy shop',
which sometimes sold clay pipes to the bairns 'for blowing
bubbles'. Come to think of it, that *might* have been a 'good
going line' if she had thought of it in the days when clay pipes cost
two for a tanner but she hadn't thought about it then, content
enough to 'carry' birds flying on a stick, for it was essential
to win access to the Mothers through an approach to their
bairns – 'You'll never die as long as that bairnie lives!' she
would assure the Mothers. 'For she carries you in her face. God
bless her. A bonnie bairn, a bonnie bairnie right enough. And

not to be wondered at, mistress! For it's a fine figure of a woman you are, *yoursel'*!'

Cursing and wheedling. The two-toned voice of her lifetime. One for her protection. T'other for her livelihood. She was not a religious woman. Not what you'd describe as 'a Christian'. Yet she had an almost 'on speaking terms' relationship with that being on whom she always laid possessive claim as '*my* maker'. His emissary, in a manner of speaking, bestowing His blessing here, His curses there. Prodigal with both.

Her tones losing something of their certitude with the passing of the years. Wheedling coming slower to the tongue. No longer setting off 'on the Toby', taking to the road in the high hope of 'wheezing the Manashees for Jowldie'. Her mind lingered momentarily, lovingly, on her own language, 'the cant'. She *herself* could still 'jan the cant.' But she had outlived her own kind who could interpret it. Their descendents couldn't. *That* was what compulsory education had done to *them*! Deprived them of their own language! Spitting out her contempt, sucking fiercely on the stub of her clay pipe, she listened to the clash and clang of the berry pickers' cans in the distance. Bramble time, she realised, staring at the bushes which surrounded her. The turn of the year taking her almost by surprise. Her attitude to the countryside she knew so well was one-dimensional. Not for *her* acclamation at the sight of the first snowdrop of spring, the wild briar roses of summer, the turning of the leaves, or the first fall of snow. She lived, without comment, within the whole. Brambles were but incidental. A thing in the passing. It was the wide berry-picking days of her youth that came to mind, filling it with a small, distinct, living clarity.

The mare hitched to the float, the 'sheltie' trotting behind it, taking herself, her man, her bairns, the whole caboodle of them,

southwards to the lush fruit-growing lands of Blairgowrie and
Dundee.

> Says I ma young lassie
> I canna weel tell ye
> I canna weel show ye
> The road ye maun gae . . .

The old ballad defied her vocal-chords, but lilted in her
memory.

> But if ye wull permit me
> tae walk along wi ye
> I'll show you the road
> And the miles tae Dundee . . .

If God, Himself, was to ask her happiest recollection of a long life,
the answer would fall quick to her tongue – 'the berry-picking,
maister'. Stripping the bushes in the warm sun. Sure of a wage at
the end of a day. Her man and his ferret away in search of a rabbit
for the pot, and all that was needed to accompany it that 'fell' to
his hand on the way. Floury tatties fresh from the field. And a
fine, sweet turnip. And aye a copper in the pocket for 'the wine
that maketh glad the heart of man'. All the same, she remembered wryly, when the drink was in, the wit went out. As it
always did at reunions with her own kind on their 'social'
occasions. At the berry-picking. Funerals. Weddings. And the
great yearly horse sale up Foggie Loan way. All ending in a
'barney', a free-for-all. No head too hard to break in *those* days.
Nor too soft to heal again.

A thing of the past now, though, the berry-picking. Students
had taken it over from her kind. But she could still teach *them* a
trick or two of the berry-picking trade. For there was more than
one way of increasing the weight of the berries in your basket
before sidling up for the 'official' weight-in. And she knew them
all.

Still, peering through the smoke rising from her pipe, in search of some other landscape, she was certain of one thing – she'd live the same life over if she had to live again. And the chances were she'd go where most men go.

The hooter from the tweed mill, sounding its cry of Release! across the countryside, broke through her sleep and startled her into consciousness. Struggling to her feet, she began to rive her way through the maze of bramble bushes. Gasping as she reached the slope of the bank, halting to catch her breath before beginning the climb.

Kirstac.

Her name reached her mind from a long way off.

'MacWhirdie Kirstac! STAND ALOFT! HALT!' Words that never age. Never tire. Never go doddering past in clichés. But are always sudden. And alive with blinding power.

'As sure as death', 'As God's my judge' . . . The vows of a lifetime that had fallen so easily from her tongue. Lending truth to the lie . . . *so*. Death *was* 'sure'. God *did* 'judge'. And this, she recognised, was *His* day.

'Move yourself, woman!' A man's voice snapped, as he nudged her towards his companion, who stood flicking through the pages of a large ledger.

'That's the lot for the day, Recorder,' he announced. 'But there's always the *one*,' he grumbled, rattling his keys against the old tinker's ears, 'always the one who arrives at the last minute! Holding everything and everybody up.'

'Patience, Peter,' his companion advised, without looking up from the ledger. 'Patience.'

'She was always the same!' A woman's voice rose up in accusation.

'That wife from the tobacconist's shop!' The tinker recognised the voice and the form, visible now through the mist beginning to clear before her eyes. *This* then was how she had always imagined Judgement Day to be. On the threshold of heaven – or hell – with all the people whose lives had brushed against her own. Had touched her. Affected her. For good or ill.

'Always the same!' The tobaconist's wife was grumbling on. 'Banging on my shop door the moment I put the shutters up for the night. Demanding – *demanding*, mind you! – half-an-ounce of bogie twist. No please or thank you. Never a 'sorry' nor a 'beg your pardon'. And the *language* that was on her! Enough to blow your *ears* off!'

'Liar!' the tinker protested, before turning to the Recorder. Contemplating him. Considering the form of address most complimentary to *him*, most favourable to *herself*. Maister . . . Sir . . . Your Honour . . . 'Your *worship*! *This* was the way of it. I'd be hawking all day for a crust. Up Moss of Barmuckity way. A God-forsaken hole of a place. As fine you know, sir. You could walk there for miles without running into a soul who could give you the time of day. So, how in God's name was *I* to know it would be closing-times before I got back?'

'Blaspheming again!' The man called Peter turned to the Recorder. 'Blasphemy! Take a note of that!'

'Anything you say,' the Recorder warned her, 'will be taken down and . . .'

' . . .used in evidence against me,' she concluded his statement for him. 'I *know*,' she admitted ruefully, memories of her 'appearances' in the police courts still in her memory, 'I know . . .'

Turning her attention to the groups in front of her, she felt her heart lift in recognition of the fish wives from the Broch. 'Souls'. Their heads covered with their black shawls, bending beneath their creels. Their red flannel skirts swaying beneath their dark aprons. Of her kind. In their own way. Striding the same country roads. Supplying the same customers. Their sing-song morning greetings in passing. 'It's threatening rain.' 'It's promising fair.'

'BUY my caller Herrin!

> 'They're bonnie Fish
> And dainty Farin
> BUY
>   My caller Herrin . . .'

But *then*! Whoever heard of a fish wife shouting 'stinking fish'? The idea of that creased her old face into a smile. 'GOOD souls.' Often taking time for a bit of barter on the road. Three herrings for a packet of needles. 'And here's yin *extra*. Thrown in for – Hansel!' For a gift.

Even so, she noticed. Here, at heaven's gate itself, the others stood apart from the fish wives. Their 'smell', she supposed. Just as the accusation of 'smell' had always kept folk from too close an approach to herself.

'No cleaner wives walks the face of this earth than the fish wives.' She heard herself exhorting the crowd. 'So you needna all stand there clutching at your skirts! The fish wives will no contaminate you! They're *clean* folk.! As clean and clear and trig as the herrins in their creels!'

'Contempt of court!' Peter rattled his keys in warning.

'AGE?' The Recorder demanded. 'Date of birth?' Her usual reply to that question was, she realised in good time, not in keeping with her present surroundings. 'As old as my tongue. And a bit older than my teeth.' Although that indeed was all she *did* know about her age. '*That*', she admitted, 'is one thing I canna tell you. I was never registered, you see.'

'Not *baptised*!' Peter's voice shook with shock. 'This woman,' he informed the Recorder, 'has surely arrived here by some gross error on somebody's part. Not baptised!'

'It does sometimes happen,' the Recorder conceded. 'We are still somewhat fallible. Watch and pray, Peter,' he reminded the man with the keys. A small smirk crossing his face as he did so. 'We still must needs watch and pray.'

'I *can* tell you one thing though,' The tinker remembered.
Anxious to please the Recorder. 'My father fought at the Battle of
Balaclava. If *that's* any help to you. Or so he claimed. Though,
truth to tell, you could never believe a word that came out of his
head.'

'*We* are well aware of *that*!' Peter snapped. 'Get on with it!'

'But *you* know my age.' She turned to the Recorder in an instant
of sudden awareness. 'You know everything.'

'A matter of form,' he said, irritation creeping into his tone.
'Simply a matter of form. Place of birth?' he demanded.

'The Glens of Foudland, sir!' *That* was what she *did* know. Not
that she, herself, remembered. But she had heard tell of it often
enough from her mother. 'At the tattie lifting. October, Novem-
ber that would be. *There*'s a date for you, Maister. A bit of a date
onywye. My mother, God rest her, just flung down her pail when
her pains came on her. Took herself over to the dyke. And I was
born in the ley of the dyke. She washed me in the burn, wrapped
me in her shawl. And was back working in the tattie drill within
an hour of my birth. We never lookit on birth as an illness, you
see.'

'And that's a fact!' Dod McCluskey the poacher snarled from
within the crowd. '*Her* kind breed like *rabbits*!'

'He kens a lot about *rabbits*!' she informed the Recorder.
'BUT!' She turned to confront the poacher. 'You ken damn all
about *tinkers*! *I* ken enough about YOU to send you straight to
HELL!' She'd said the *right* thing, but realising that she'd said it
in the *wrong* place at the wrong time, she struggled to contain her
rising anger.

'However mony bairns *we* brought into this weary world,' she
conceded. 'And I'll no deny *that*. We lippened on no man for help
to rear them. *We* never "signed on the broo", applied for the
means test. Nor did we ever "line up" for "chits" for free boots.
Free clothes for *our* bairns! As this man beside me' – she turned to
the Recorder – 'can vouch for! *Our* folk never had to end their

days deserted. Up yonder in the poor's house! They got the *dignity* of dying in their own beds. In the tent or wagon that was their home. Nor did *they* end up in a pauper's grave. Our tribe made sure of *that*! Each according to what he could afford!

'*Another* thing, Dod.' She paused, struggling with the anger again, threatening to overcome her. 'We *knew* that our husbands, our *men*, had fathered *our* bairns. For our women marry virgin. That was the law. And no very often broken! So that we *knew*. Aye! And our *husbands* knew. It takes a wise man to know his own, as the good man standing beside me will agree! So, you see, Dod, I wonder, I wonder if *you* ever took a good look at that last littl'un o' yours, the wee red-heided lad. Him that's the living spit o' Chae Tastard, the coalman. "Ripe ripe like a cherry, ready to burst" – *that* was aye what Chae had to say about *your* wife, in The Hole In the Wall on a Saturday night. Mind *you*! He *could* have been exaggerating! With a good drink inside o' him. He *must* have been!' The image of Dod's great slorach of a wife rising up in her vision. 'Some CHERRY!' she chuckled.

'Contempt of court.' Peter shouted, as the crowd joined in her laughter.

'*ADULTERY*!' he prompted, peering over the Recorder's shoulder to examine the ledger.

'*That*,' the Recorder pointed out, 'has just been dealt with, in some detail.'

'BEGGING?'

'Not,' the Recorder informed him, 'included in the Ten Commandments.'

'A pity that,' Peter grumbled. 'We *know* that the Defendant was guilty enough of *that*!'

'Thou shalt not covet'. COVET. Aware of the blank expression on the Tinker's face, the Recorder turned towards her in explanation. 'COVET. To want to possess that which belongs to another human being.'

'When I was a young woman, sir,' – her words came out of

long, backward reflection – 'and had just got married on to Donald McWhirdie, I had a sore hankering for a van with a wooden roof. Like the one my good-mother (mother-in-law) lived in. We had just got a wagon, you see. With the old tarpaulin covering. Green, it was. But I would have liked a van with a wooden roof. "You'll manage to get one through time," my good-mother said. Oh! We *did* get one. We got one . . . "through time." But, it's the long wait through time that claws at your gut, when you're young. But Maister – Gospel Truth! – I never grudged my good-mother *her* van with a wooden roof. I never cast my eye on that!'

'FALSE WITNESS. Thou shalt not bear . . .'

'Many a time that. But,' she qualified, 'only when false witness was born against *me*. And *that* happened more times than I can count!'

'An eye for an eye,' the Recorder murmured.

'Whiles, of course,' she continued, 'whiles, I'd stand up in the court and lie till I was blue in the face. For my man. Poachin' was *his* trouble. Oh! but he could net a salmon. Up at the Brig o' Feuch, yonder. He could *that*! And *that* was something to *see*, sir! The salmon rinnin' and leaping for life. The thing was he, himsel aye got catched! An impatient chield, my man. Reckless, when it came to poaching. Could never wait for the dark night. Never him! But up and off when the moon was full. And the countryside as bright as day. I would swear in the court that he had never left his bed, in hope of mistaken identity. But no other man born was *his* marrow! You could never mistake *him* for anybody else. You can do no *less*, maister, no less than stick up your *ain* man. And if *that's* false witness, then I'm guilty o't.'

'FALSE PRETENCES.' The Recorder turned towards her. 'Gaining money by false pretences.'

'And *that's* true enough!' A voice full of remembered grievance rose up in accusation. 'That old *tink* did *that* right enough!'

Peering forward, she recognised her accuser – Teen Slater, yon simple craittur that was servant at the farm-toun of Drumlogie.

'Many a bonnie penny she did *me* for!' Teen complained. 'Her and her promises. Her and her lies! "A bittie o' silver tae cross her palm," she's wheedle. Forbye! Scrounging a cup of tea to read the leaves. A tall dark man she promised *me*! Weel set up wi' gear and plenishings, she said! Time and time again, at a tanner a time! She promised *me*! And wha did *I* end up wi'? Jeems Simmers. Yon wee bauchle. Him that was orra man at the fornet. Wi no twa coppers to jingle together!'

'And if it wasna' the teacups,' an anonymous voice cried from the crowd, 'it was the white heather! "White heather to bring you luck", was *that* one's cry. Waving it in front o your nose. Near forcing't on you! *White* heather. Some white heather. Just a wheen faded dirt from the Moss o' Barmuckity.'

'*One* minute! A *minute* just!' The tinker's protest rang round the gates of heaven. 'One minute, sir'. She turned to the Recorder. 'Begging your pardon, maister. I *did* read the cups. But I was always persuaded, bribed, by the country lassies and wives to "read their fortunes." Mistress and her maid were the same in *that* respect. I never laid claim of having the gift to see into the future. That was forced upon me. *They* had the idea in their *ain* heads, that, being a tinker, I could read their fortunes. That's the burden of being a tinker. Folk get by-ordinar notions about you. And, truth to tell, as time passes you almost believe them yoursel! *One* thing though, maister. All I ever *did* tell them was the things I knew they wanted to hear. So. I'd give them good health. A handsome man. A bairn or two. And a full purse. I *never* sent them away wi' a sore heart! Surely, sir, that was worth a tanner! As for the heather, I plead guilty to that. Only I never asked a penny for my offering. Nor forced it on them. Their own superstition did that.'

'THOU SHALT NOT STEAL'.

'Many's the autumn,' the blacksmith's wife from Corrieben began to testify, '*that* one picked the gooseberries growing at the back of my house. Then had the bare-faced cheek to *sell* them at *me* front door! I never caught her at it. She'd skedaddled down the road before I noticed that my bushes were stripped clean!'

'You *must* answer,' The Recorder urged, breaking into her thoughts. '*Did* you, or did you *not*?'

'You *ken* I did! Although I never looked on it as theft *myself*. I never charged the wumman for her *ain* gooseberries. I only asked for a copper or two for *picking* them for her! That seemed to *me* a fair enough exchange.'

'NOT PROVEN!' Peter glared at the ticket in his hand. 'Impossible!' he shouted to the Recorder. 'There's a mistake on somebody's part. A *mistake*, I tell you!'

'No mistake,' the Recorder assured him. 'The verdict came direct from Himself. And, as *we* know, Peter, as we know, He works in a mysterious way.'

Wordlessly Peter handed the ticket to the old tinker. No confession, it seemed to *her*, as she twirled the ticket in her hands, was so shameful, so demanding as the one that *now* faced her. That she couldn't write had never bothered her. 'X' had covered and contained the few, official documents of her lifetime. But reading, not to be able to read . . . 'Would you' – she turned to the Recorder – 'be a good soul and tell me what the ticket says. I canna see without my specs. And I've left them down in my basket.'

> Admit BEARER Heavenwards.
> East Open Stand. North End
>   Row 11
>   Seat 12

The disappointment that struck at her heart sounded itself in her voice. 'Is *that* all it is! I was hoping it was a ticket for a bed for the night in the Corporation lodging-house.'